Sparrow Road

Sparrow Road

SHEILA O'CONNOR

PUFFIN BOOKS
An Imprint of Penguin Group (USA) Inc.

PUFFIN BOOKS

Published by the Penguin Group

Penguin Young Readers Group, 345 Hudson Street, New York, New York 10014, U.S.A.

Penguin Group (Canada), 90 Eglinton Avenue East, Suite 700, Toronto, Ontario, Canada M4P 2Y3
(a division of Pearson Penguin Canada Inc.)

Penguin Books Ltd, 80 Strand, London WC2R 0RL, England

Penguin Ireland, 25 St Stephen's Green, Dublin 2, Ireland (a division of Penguin Books Ltd)

Penguin Group (Australia), 250 Camberwell Road, Camberwell, Victoria 3124, Australia
(a division of Pearson Australia Group Pty Ltd)

Penguin Books India Pvt Ltd, 11 Community Centre,
Panchsheel Park, New Delhi - 110 017, India

Penguin Group (NZ), 67 Apollo Drive, Rosedale, Auckland 0632, New Zealand
(a division of Pearson New Zealand Ltd.)

Penguin Books (South Africa) (Pty) Ltd, 24 Sturdee Avenue,
Rosebank, Johannesburg 2196, South Africa

Registered Offices: Penguin Books Ltd, 80 Strand, London WC2R 0RL, England

First published in the United States of America by G. P. Putnam's Sons, a division of
Penguin Young Readers Group, 2011
Published by Puffin Books, a division of Penguin Young Readers Group, 2012

3 5 7 9 10 8 6 4

THE LIBRARY OF CONGRESS HAS CATALOGED THE G. P. PUTNAM'S SONS EDITION AS FOLLOWS:

O'Connor, Sheila.
Sparrow Road / Sheila O'Connor.
p. cm.
Summary: Twelve-year-old Raine spends the summer at a mysterious artists' colony and discovers a
secret about her past.
ISBN: 978-0-399-25458-1 (hc)
[1. Artists colonies—Fiction. 2. Secrets—Fiction.]
I. Title
PZ7.O22264Sp 2011
[Fic]—dc22 2010028290

Puffin Books ISBN 978-0-14-242136-9

Design by Marikka Tamura
Set in Centaur

Printed in the United States of America

What mysteries are in town?

"Mama, what's in Comfort?" I asked her the next day.

We were stretched out on a blanket at the lake with a picnic lunch of ham sandwiches, ripple chips, and pickles.

"Stores and things." Mama flushed. "Nothing really, Raine."

"And you go there to buy groceries?" Both times Mama had gone to town with Viktor she'd brushed her curls, put on clean clothes and earrings like there was more to Comfort than shopping for our food. And both times she'd come back with fluster blotches burning on her neck.

"I do," Mama said. "Why the questions, Raine? You've seen the bags yourself. You've helped unload the groceries."

"I know." I had, but there was something suspicious about her trips to town with Viktor. Like her sudden summer job at Sparrow Road, Mama's answers didn't add up. No matter how many times I asked.

OTHER BOOKS YOU MAY ENJOY

Beloved children

~

I give you Sparrow Road

In the shadowed glow of headlights the old pink house looked huge, rambling like the mansions on Lake Michigan. A fairy-tale tower rose high above the roof. The pillared front porch sagged.

"However humble," Viktor said. He steered his truck to a slow stop. "I give you Sparrow Road."

"*You* own this place?" I gasped. Viktor's rusted truck reeked of mud and grease; his sunken face was covered in white whiskers. He looked too poor to own a country mansion, even one as worn as this was.

"Raine!" Mama jabbed her elbow in my ribs. "Viktor owns the whole estate."

"The main house," Viktor said as if he hadn't heard me, "is where the artists sleep. Your cottage is a short walk through the meadow." It was the most I'd heard him say since he met us at our train.

"Well, it's nothing like Milwaukee, that's for sure." Mama gave me a weak smile.

1

Just hearing Mama say *Milwaukee* made me miss it more. Already our apartment seemed another world away, a place where Grandpa Mac waited, lonesome with us gone. I thought of Grandpa Mac standing sad-eyed at the station, the secret fifty-dollar bill he stashed in my back pocket. *In case of an emergency*, he warned, like he knew one was ahead.

"I would assume"—Viktor cleared his throat as if those few words wore him out—"the four artists are asleep at this late hour." Only one small curtained window was lit up in the house. He opened up his truck door. "I shall get your bags."

"I don't want to stay," I said the second Viktor left us in the truck. Sparrow Road looked haunted-mansion creepy, the same way Viktor Berglund looked when I saw him at the train. A man so thin he looked more skeleton than human; a man with ice blue eyes and a face as cold as stone.

Mama touched my cheek. "Sweetheart, we can't leave."

"Grandpa Mac said he'd come to get me. Day or night. All I have to do is call. We can go back to the station, wait there for a train." I still had the good-bye apple muffins Grandpa baked us in my backpack. A bag of wilted grapes. Grandpa's fifty-dollar bill.

"We can't," Mama said. "And Grandpa Mac is far away. For the first time in a long time, it's only you and me." She wove her sweaty fingers between mine.

Your mother's done some crazy things, but this? Suddenly Grandpa Mac's worries were moving into mine.

"But you don't even like to clean," I said. Grandpa Mac always joked that Mama's middle name was Mess. Now I'd lose what was left of my good summer so Mama could cook and keep house for some artists in the country.

"Raine," Mama said. "We've been over this already. A hundred times at least."

We had. Still, none of Mama's reasons for this job made an ounce of sense to me. "But Sparrow Road?" I said. "You had a job back in Milwaukee."

"Sweetheart," Mama said. She opened up the truck door. "This is going to take some brave from both of us."

It took more than brave for me to follow brooding Viktor across the dew-soaked meadow. It took Mama's hand clenched around my elbow and a night so black I was too afraid to stay in Viktor's truck all by myself.

"The bats," Viktor warned. "Don't be startled by the swoops."

I pressed in close to Mama. A symphony of insects rattled in the grass. "Are there snakes?" I asked.

"Raine's used to the city," Mama said to Viktor.

Even the country air smelled strange. A mix of fresh-cut grass and lilacs, rotten apples, raspberries, and pine. Maybe fish, like a lake might be nearby.

"And to think," Mama said like she hoped to get some happy conversation started. "Just three days ago, I was serving lunch to crabby customers at Christos."

"Three days ago," I added, "I was stacking shelves at Grandpa's store." All the Popsicles and candy I could eat. Our portable TV tucked behind the counter. Brewers' games on Grandpa Mac's transistor. Chess with Grandpa's best friend, Mr. Sheehan, when the afternoons got long. The summer job I loved, and Mama made me leave it.

"Oh, Raine." Mama faked a cheery laugh. "You spend every summer in that store. Besides, we'll only be here a few weeks."

"Eight," I moaned. "If you make us stay until September."

Mama gave my arm a sharp, be-quiet squeeze. "Raine's tired," Mama said, like I was six instead of twelve. "Ten hours on a train. That long ride from the station. She needs to get some sleep."

Sleep. I wasn't going to sleep a wink at Sparrow Road. Grandpa Mac always said he couldn't get to sleep without the song of sirens, the noise of neighbors humming through our walls, the roar of city traffic on the street. It would be the same for me.

"Tomorrow," Viktor said, "I shall take you on a tour. Tomorrow is a Sunday. On Sundays we may speak."

"Speak?" I said.

"As I explained," he said to Mama, "every day is silent until supper. Every day but Sunday."

"What?" I said. "Silent until supper?"

"I assumed she knew the rules," Viktor said like his mouth was dry with dust.

"She does," Mama lied. She tried to nudge me forward, but I wouldn't take another step. A thick swarm of mosquitoes feasted on my skin. Tomorrow I'd be covered in red welts.

"I don't." I slapped down at my leg. "Mama never mentioned any rules."

"Just a few," Mama said. No one hated rules more than Mama. "Like there won't be any newspapers."

"Is that it?" I asked. No newspapers was nothing like silence until supper.

"Or television," Viktor said to Mama. "Or radio. Or music. Not at any time."

"What?" I said. "No TV until September? No radio? And we can't even talk?"

"Molly," Viktor said. "If it's a problem for the child?"

"It is," I answered.

"Raine's not a child," Mama said. "She'll make it through just fine."

"The artists," Viktor said, "they require quiet. They only have the summer for their work. As it is, it's already July."

I wasn't going to talk to any artists. The second I saw daylight I was calling Grandpa Mac. Collect. Just the way he taught me.

"Of course," Mama agreed. "We won't disturb the artists. We'll have enough to keep us busy, as you know."

"Let us hope," Viktor said.

"As for the rules," Mama added quickly, "we completely understand."

"I don't," I said again. "I don't understand at all."

Our cottage was a tiny Snow White house where a gardener used to sleep. Inside it smelled like dust balls and old clothes;—abandoned, like no one had lived in it for years. There was a sunken couch, a painted wooden rocker, and a little purple table just for two.

"Well, it's cute," Mama said when Viktor left.

"Cute?" The walls were butter yellow, the white lace curtains grayed. "Maybe in a rundown dollhouse kind of way." I rolled my eyes at Mama. I didn't care about the cottage. "No TV? Silence until supper? All those stupid rules you didn't tell me?"

"I was going to," Mama said. "Just not on our first day." She wiped her palm across the dusty table. "Don't worry, Raine, we'll make it our own place."

The only place I wanted was Milwaukee. I lugged my suitcase up the narrow staircase to the tiny slanted bedroom where Viktor told us we would sleep. Heat pressed down from the ceiling; a hint of breeze blew through the open window.

"How is it?" Mama asked, but I didn't answer.

It was daisy wallpaper peeled away in patches, two sagging beds, a broken mirror nailed to the wall. I flopped down on the musty mattress, hugged a flimsy pillow to my chest. At home, Beauty would be purring on my bed. Grandpa Mac would be watching some old western on TV.

"Love you to the moon and back," I whispered to Grandpa Mac. It's what I always said before I went to bed. A single tear trickled down my cheek. *Love you to the stars,* he said to me. *Good night, sweet girl. I'll see you in my dreams.*

The strange thing is, I slept. Long and deep, the way I sometimes did with fevers. When I woke up the next morning the spicy smell of coffee filled the cottage and Mama's bed was made.

"Mama?" I called. She never made her bed.

"Down here, sleepyhead," Mama almost sang. "Come see, Raine. I've been cleaning up our cottage. And everything looks better with the sun."

Downstairs, Mama sat at the little purple table—her long red curls still wet from washing, her denim overalls rolled up to her knees. The smell of dust had already disappeared. Warm white light poured through the open windows. "Getting ready for our week." Mama patted a stack of yellowed cookbooks. "I found these in the cupboard. The birds wouldn't let me sleep."

I slumped down in the chair and wiped the sleep out of my eyes. "I need a phone," I said. "This morning."

"There's no phone, Raine. I'm sorry." But sorry wasn't in her voice.

"No phone?" I looked around the cottage. "No phones at Sparrow Road?"

Mama shook her head. "The artists come to Sparrow Road to get away."

"Right. No talking. No TV." I dropped my head into my hands. Six days a week of silence, now I couldn't even find a phone. "But what about emergencies? A fire? Some-one could get hurt." I was two when Grandpa Mac taught me how to phone for help.

"In an emergency," Mama said, "I'm sure a call can be arranged."

"Okay," I said. "It's an emergency today."

Mama stared into my eyes. "This isn't an emergency. It's change. I know that you're unhappy, but we'll get used to it. We will."

"But why?"

Mama turned the pages of her cookbook like an answer would be there. "I told you, Raine, I came to do a job."

"You had a job at Christos."

"Another job," Mama said. "A job that wasn't in Mil-waukee. And I'll have my Christos job when we go home." She slapped the cookbook shut. "Raine," she sighed, "not everything's a mystery." It's what she always said when she was tired of my questions or when she held a secret she wasn't going to tell.

"I know," I said. "Not everything. But this?" Our move to Sparrow Road was a mystery to me.

"But hey!" Suddenly she jumped up and an unexpected smile lit up her worried face. "If you're looking for a mystery, I've got a real one you can solve." She grabbed my wrist and pulled me toward the counter. "Look!" she cried. "Like Easter!"

Underneath a drape of emerald velvet was a lilac wicker basket filled with water-colored eggs, a jelly jar of flowers, warm banana bread, and two small tangerines. On a torn scrap of paper WELCOME had been glued in golden glitter. "I found it here this morning, at our door."

"Weird," I said. "Viktor didn't make this."

"No," Mama said. "I don't think so either." I heard a hint of wonder in her voice. Like maybe something was a mystery to her. "And this?" Mama handed me a linen napkin, white, with the towered house embroidered in the center and my initials *R.O.* stitched into the corner. "There's a second one for me," Mama said.

"So someone knows our names," I said. "Someone besides Viktor."

"Yes," Mama said. "Someone who must be happy that we're here."

Mama was right. Sparrow Road looked different in the sunlight. Outside, miles of rolling hills formed a patchwork quilt of green, wildflowers swayed graceful in the meadow, and the sky seemed to stretch forever in a perfect, deep blue sea. It was a pretty place I might have loved with Grandpa Mac and Mama. A vacation place without Viktor and his rules, and all the silent days I had ahead.

When Viktor came to take us on the tour, I let Mama walk beside him. I was happiest a few steps back, away from Viktor's stony quiet, his icy eyes, his sunken face covered in white whiskers. Plus there was something I was watching—the friendly way they talked, the way Mama seemed too sweet, too comfortable with a man as cold as Viktor. Too at home, like she and Viktor knew each other before he met us at the train.

He led us down a steep path to a lake. "Sorrow Lake," he wheezed when we'd made it to the shore. "But here, I need a rest." He sat down in the shade while Mama and I left him for the dock.

"Sorrow Lake?" I said to Mama, when I was sure Viktor was too far away to eavesdrop. "Isn't that a strange name? And how can Viktor own a lake? No one owns Lake Michigan."

Mama shook her head. "So many questions, Raine."

"Did you know Viktor before he got us at the train?"

"Know him?" Mama closed her eyes, tilted her face up toward the sun. "Viktor hired me. It's how I got the job."

"But did you know him in Milwaukee? Or some time before now?"

Mama opened up one eye and gave me a mean squint.

"You just seem to know him, like he might be your friend."

"Viktor is my boss." Too many questions got on Mama's nerves. "I'm here to work for him."

I slipped off my flip-flops and dipped my toes into the lake. A school of minnows skittered near the surface. "So can we swim after the tour?" I wanted something happy up ahead, something besides Viktor's boring tour and Mama planning out her menu for the week.

"We'll see." A flush of red washed over Mama's face. Already, her pale Irish skin burned a little pink. I didn't have Mama's coloring or beauty. I was dark-eyed, dark-skinned, with straight black hair, and skinny, where Mama was all curves. "This afternoon," Mama said, "I need to go with Viktor into Comfort."

"Comfort?"

"It's a town not far away. It's where I'll buy the groceries."

"You? You mean you're going without me?"

Mama kept her eyes closed. "Viktor's truck," she said. "There isn't really room for three."

"There were three of us last night." We were crowded knee to knee, but we still fit.

"Another time. Today you'll have to stay here by yourself."

"Alone? At Sparrow Road? Mama, there's nothing here for miles except for hills!"

"The artists," Mama said, although we hadn't seen them. "Surely one of them would be near if some emergency occurred." Sparrow Road had cast some kind of crazy spell on Mama. At home Mama worried when I walked six blocks to the library. Mama always acted like I'd be snatched off of some street. Grandpa Mac did, too. Now she was going to leave me in the country by myself?

"I want to go with you. There's room for me in Viktor's truck."

"No." Mama stood, then offered me a hand. "I'm afraid today I'll need to go with Viktor."

By the time we finally made it to the main house, I was too mad at Mama to listen to Viktor's dull descriptions. Instead I kept my eyes out for an artist, someone who'd be nearby at least while Mama was in town.

"Well, it certainly is spotless," Mama said the minute we stepped inside the house. I could tell she was relieved.

It was almost spooky clean, like a house where no one lived. The dark woodwork was all polished, floors and ceiling beams and benches. Crystal chandeliers sparkled in the sun. It smelled like Holy Trinity, our church back in Milwaukee—hot candle wax and lemon polish, a trace of sweet perfume. A wide, grand wooden staircase curved up from the front room.

Viktor cleared his throat. "The artists keep it tidy." He raised his lanky arm and pointed down a hallway. "Our poet, Lillian Hobbs, has the room off of the library."

"A poet?" Mama said, surprised. "How nice. Raine writes."

"I wrote," I said. "In fourth grade." Back when my teacher, Sister Cyril, told me to put my imagination to good use. But I didn't want Mama to tell my past to Viktor. Not a word.

"Our other summer artists—Josie, Eleanor, Diego— all reside upstairs. And each one has a shed where they create. Although Lillian and Eleanor often work here in their rooms." He'd already pointed out the little sheds as we'd walked across the meadow. Two in the tall grass. Two tucked back in the woods. "Of course the artists' sheds, their rooms, all those spaces are totally off-limits. Always. Like the silence until supper; that rule must be honored. The artists came for quiet. They must be left alone."

Viktor made it sound like every rule was for me, like there was no place for a kid at Sparrow Road.

"We understand," Mama said. I could tell she wanted to get Viktor off the rules.

"And here"—Viktor led us to a gleaming tiled kitchen where copper pots hung from silver hooks—"is where you shall prepare the evening meals. As you wished."

"You *wished* to make the meals?" I asked Mama, but Mama just ignored me.

"Every day but Sunday," Viktor said. "On Sundays you are free."

The smell of peanut butter and warm toast lingered in the kitchen. Maple syrup that reminded me of home. Earlier, an artist must have eaten breakfast. I wondered where they were this morning, what they looked like, if one of them would be here when Mama went to town. Close enough to help if something happened?

And which one left that basket at our door?

Mama ordered me to lock the door and stay put in our cottage, but the minute I heard Viktor's rusted truck rumble from the driveway, I headed toward the main house to wait out on the porch. Even if the artists were all strangers, I felt safer near my neighbors, the way we lived at home.

I perched on the weathered porch swing, gave it one good push until it swayed. I couldn't believe Mama went off to town with Viktor. My first letter home, I'd write it all to Grandpa Mac; I'd tell him how she left me my first day. How she took me to a place where I couldn't speak.

"Oh my." A wobbly, weak-bird voice floated through the window. "Another child left here all alone." The front door opened, then slapped closed. A tiny, frail woman shuffled toward the swing. "I'm Lillian Hobbs, dear girl."

Lillian? The poet Viktor mentioned on the tour?

"I'm Raine," I said. "Raine O'Rourke."

Lillian reached down and brushed her hand over my shoulder. "Dear child, did you come here for a home?"

"No," I said. "I'm just waiting for my mother."

"I'm sure," Lillian said. "All our children are." She shook her head. "I hope you're not too scared."

"No," I lied, "not really." Twelve was too old to admit to being scared, even if all the empty in the country scared me some.

"Well, good for you. You're brave." Lillian was old. Not old like Grandpa Mac or Viktor, but a fragile, feeble old I hoped I'd never be. "May I join you on the porch swing?" she asked. "Perhaps a friend would help."

Even though Mama warned me not to interrupt the artists, Lillian was the one who interrupted me. I hadn't done a thing but sit outside. "Sure." I held the porch swing steady. "Be careful sitting down."

When she finally settled safely on the swing her little legs dangled in midair. She was child-small, with snowy hair that fell softly to her shoulders and skin so thin I could almost see her bones. She smelled like powder and sweet soap.

"Sad?" She made a little frown.

"No." I was mad and sad, homesick and suspicious, with a mix of other feelings in between. "Mostly I'm just waiting."

"Of course." She smoothed her flowered dress against her lap. "The other children? Do you know where they've gone?"

"Children? I think I'm the only child here."

"Oh no, dear." Lillian patted at my leg. "You'll see them soon enough. Perhaps they're down at Sorrow Lake. Sometimes at night the children sleep there in this heat."

"No," I said. "There were no children there."

She gave me a sweet smile. "You won't be alone here. You'll have a happy home at Sparrow Road. Everyone is scared in the beginning."

"The beginning?" Lillian made it sound like I'd come to live forever. "I'm just here until September," I said. Mama promised Grandpa Mac.

"We all like to think so." Her pebbled eyes were milky. "We may not be your family, but we'll try our best to be."

"Thanks," I said. "But I already have a family." I had Grandpa Mac and Mama, but right now both of them were gone.

"Yes," she said, "everybody does." She pulled a pack of faded kid's cards from her pocket. "Old Maid?" she asked. "It seems to be the one game the new ones always know. Especially a girl your age."

A girl my age knew more games than Old Maid; I hadn't played Old Maid since I was little. "Sure." I shrugged. Any game was better than sitting in our cottage all alone.

Lillian reached back into her pocket, fished out a linty lemon drop, and handed it to me. "Sugar," she cooed. "It helps to heal the heart."

•••

The two of us played Old Maid on the splintered picnic table with the tinkle of pink shell chimes clinking in the breeze. In between hands Lillian sent me inside the silent house for warm apple juice and crackers. A kind of kindergarten snack that reminded me of days when I was small.

When we got tired of Old Maid, Lillian told stories. She told me she didn't write poems until after she was sixty, and that this summer she'd come here from a horrible high-rise for seniors in St. Paul. A room so far above the earth she wasn't sure most days if she was already in heaven. She told me she had taught piano to 237 students, and that Viktor Berglund was a prodigy, a child who studied music with the masters in Vienna. A composer. She said Viktor brought her here this summer to put more poems on paper.

"They're all right here." She tapped her wrinkled finger on her heart. "I carry them inside me. I don't need to write them down." Then she leaned forward and lowered her weak voice to a whisper. "Please don't tell that to Viktor." She looked back at the house to make sure no one was watching.

"Tell what?" I said. I wasn't ever going to speak to Viktor Berglund.

"I didn't come home to write poems. I came home to help the children."

"Home?" I asked. Was Sparrow Road her home? Hadn't Lillian just said that she came here from St. Paul? "The children?" I looked out toward the woods, the gravel driveway, the endless hills of green. If there were kids at Sparrow Road, I sure hadn't seen them.

"Yes." She put another lemon drop into my hand. "At Sparrow Road, the children must come first."

"Ah yes, those missing children!" A man's deep voice boomed out through the doorway. "It looks like one has finally arrived!" He was barefoot, in a tropical pink shirt and lime shorts that hung loose to his knees. He didn't look like an artist; he looked like he was headed for a beach. His smile was wide, his teeth so white they dazzled in the sun. His happy brown eyes gleamed. His wide belly and big shoulders made me think of Grandpa Mac.

"Well, good morning, lovely Lilly." He planted a loud kiss on Lillian's old cheek. Then he reached out and shook my hand. His skin was warm and soft, his handshake kind, exactly like his face. "Diego Garcia." He smiled at me. "I apologize for the appearance. Late night working in my shed."

So he really was an artist?

"I'm Raine," I said. "Raine O'Rourke. My mom's the summer—" I didn't want to say maid. Or housekeeper or cook. I didn't want Mama to be their servant. Or for me to be the daughter of the maid.

"Her mother's gone," Lillian whispered grimly. She made it sound like Mama left for good.

"She just went to town for groceries," I said quickly. Lillian patted at my leg like she thought I was confused.

"Groceries?" Diego asked. Then another lively smile covered his wide face. "Oh, I get it now! Your mother's our new chef! The one Viktor said was coming." He drummed his hand against his belly.

Chef? Mama wasn't a chef exactly, but at least it sounded better than the maid.

"We've been starving since Estelle left us in mid-June. She moved to Fargo and Viktor couldn't replace her until now. The four of us have made do on our own."

"Not starving," Lillian corrected. "No one starves at Sparrow Road."

"Right." Diego laughed. "Not if you count Josie's odd concoctions. Her horrible carrot stew. Or my dry meat-loaf. Or the applesauce you love."

"Everyone has duties," Lillian said. "I teach piano and help the children with their spelling." She looked at me. "We shall start your lessons soon."

I was a straight-A speller, but I didn't tell her that.

"You can start my lessons, Lilly." Diego winked at me like we were on the same side of a secret. "I still can't spell *Albuquerque* and I lived there as a kid."

I laughed. I couldn't spell it either. "That's like Milwaukee, where I'm from," I said. "Lots of people can't spell that."

"Milwaukee?" Diego looked surprised. "You sure came a long way." The way he said it brought the homesick straight back to my heart.

"Ten hours on a train," I said.

"All that distance just to work for Viktor?"

"I guess," I said. "Mama took the job."

"That so?" Diego sipped his coffee. "Your dad here with you, too?" I knew what he was asking, the same thing everybody asked when it was only Mama and me.

"No dad," I finally said. I tried to say it straight, confident, the way Mama always did. *No dad.* Two simple words. No other explanation, no matter who asked Mama. Even me. *No dad,* like that should be enough.

"No?" Diego frowned. "Not ever?"

I shook my head. My ears burned at the tips. I hated questions I couldn't answer. And even more I hated how often I was asked.

"I'm sure you miss him, dear," Lillian said. I was missing something but I couldn't say what it was. Or who it was exactly. A kind of puzzle piece I couldn't picture.

"Well, enough of that," Diego said. I could see that he was sorry he had asked. Lots of people were: teachers, parents, doctors. "How about we get started with my spelling? *Dumb.* D-U-M-M," Diego joked. "I should be able to spell that."

For a while we sat there in the sunlight, Diego with his coffee, Lillian quizzing us on easy words to spell. On some, like *reindeer*, I did better than Diego, and every time I did Diego laughed.

"I should go," I finally said. Happy as I was, I didn't want Viktor to come back and catch me with the artists; I didn't want to be the kid in everybody's way. "I know you need your privacy."

"Privacy?" Diego said. "It's Sunday! We have privacy all week. It's your company we need. Plus, you still need a tour of the house."

"Viktor gave us one this morning."

"Viktor's tour," Diego scoffed. "My tour is top secret. The Sparrow Road you'll never see with Viktor. Come on, let's do it while he's gone."

"I shall wait here for the others," Lillian said. "If there's an empty bed, please put her in the blue room."

"Will do." Diego winked at me again. "Don't you worry, Lilly. We'll get it all worked out."

Diego led me through the back door of the house. "This," he said, "is what we call the Secret Passage." He opened up a door to a steep, dark, narrow staircase. "The servants' entrance from the old days. It's what Josie and I take to get up to our rooms."

When we reached the second floor, I followed Diego down a hallway dim with daytime shadow, where every door was closed. From somewhere in the darkness I could hear the drone of clicks. *Click, click, click.*

"That's Eleanor." Diego rolled his eyes. "She's another writer here this summer. But nothing like sweet Lillian. All she does is type. Day and night. The good news is she rarely leaves her room. Except for dinner, you'll hardly have to see her. Just don't let her catch you roaming through the house."

"I won't," I said. I wasn't going to come up here alone.

"Here"—he tapped against a door—"is where I sleep. Most of these upstairs rooms have gone to ruin. They all need work. A house this old, it's tough to keep it up.

Viktor had some painters here, but they quit the day we came. Viktor doesn't want the restoration to interrupt the artists." He motioned down another hallway. "That's where Josie sleeps. If she sleeps." Diego laughed. "Mostly, she's in search of some adventure. Wait until you meet her, your life won't be the same."

"Does she paint eggs?" I asked. So far, I hadn't solved that mystery. And I couldn't imagine Diego embroidering those napkins. Eleanor didn't sound kind enough to leave a basket at our door.

"Eggs?" Diego raised his eyebrows.

"You know, like colored eggs for Easter?"

Diego laughed again. "I wouldn't be surprised."

I trailed him down another shadowed hallway until he stopped, reached up to a ledge, and slid down a silver key. "This little jewel," he said, grinning, "Josie just discovered! I don't know how she found it, but she did."

He slid the key into the lock and led me up another staircase. At the top was an abandoned attic room, the air so thick I could feel it in my throat. Gauzy cobwebs hung over the windows. Dust clumps littered the old floor. There were rows of metal beds, some bare down to the springs. Someone had taped kids' drawings on the walls.

The attic had the haunted feel of lives left off in the middle. "Who lived here?" I asked. "The servants?"

Diego plucked a tarnished penny off the floor and handed it to me. "Orphans," he said.

"Orphans?" Were those the children Lillian imagined? The ones who played Old Maid? The ones who slept down at the lake? "In this attic?"

Everywhere were scraps kids left behind—broken crayons, silver jacks, glass marbles. Small forgotten things that reminded me of toys I used to buy from the bubble-gum machine at Grandpa's store. Parachutes and rings and fake tattoos.

"Yep," Diego said. "Back when Viktor's great-grandsomething owned this huge estate he leased it to a charity. Folks who made a home for kids. Sparrow Road Children's Home. Josie found the nameplate in some box out in the barn."

I counted off the empty beds. Ten, twenty, thirty. "Thirty orphans?"

"Probably more," Diego said. "No question this old house had the space."

"But where did they all go?"

"Grew up." Diego wiped the sweat off of his forehead. It felt like we were roasting in an oven. "Like everybody else."

"When did they all leave?"

"That's Josie's latest mystery." Diego laughed. "She's always looking for a story. And I'm pretty sure she's going to find one here."

The whole room was a mystery—the empty beds, the drawings, the dusty trinkets some kids must have loved. I felt like if I waited long enough voices would float out of the walls. "Can't she just ask Viktor?"

"Viktor?" Diego scoffed again. "He won't talk about this place. Not any of the history. Too many old ghosts here."

"Ghosts?" Suddenly I pictured wisps of orphans swooping through the dark, slipping through our cottage walls while Mama and I slept.

"Not real ghosts," Diego said. "*Old ghosts* is a phrase. You know, like the secrets people keep. I get the feeling the orphanage is history the Iceberg would rather not remember."

"The Iceberg?"

"Oh, that's our name for Viktor. The Iceberg. Josie made it up. It's fitting, don't you think? Impenetrable. Cold."

"Yes," I said. The Iceberg was the perfect name for Viktor.

"Speaking of—" Diego squeezed my shoulder. "Let's finish off this tour before the Iceberg ends our fun."

The last stop on Diego's tour was the tower. "It looks cool from the outside," Diego said. "But it's ten times better standing at the top." He pointed to an iron ladder bolted to the wall. "With all their money, the Berglunds should've built a staircase. But you'll see it's worth the trip."

Diego cupped his hands into a stirrup for my foot. "Grab hold of that first rung and after that keep climbing."

"That's okay. I don't need to climb up to the top." I hated heights, all heights. Even monkey bars at recess. It was a safety fear passed down from Grandpa Mac and Mama. Ever since I could remember, the two of them always worried I would fall.

"Come on," Diego said. "It's totally spectacular."

"I can't," I said.

"Sure you can, it's easy. If I can do it, anybody can."

"No." I shook my head.

"It's too good to be missed. I swear it's worth it, Raine.

Here's the trick: just focus on the ceiling. One rung after the next and then you're there. I'll be right behind you all the way."

"You're sure?" Scared as I was, I reached up for that first rung. My heart raced, but still I did it. Rung after rung. The higher that I climbed, the worse the bars slipped between my sweaty fingers. Still I held on hard, because down below Diego cheered me on.

"You're almost there," he said when I made it to the top. "Give a shove to that trapdoor and push it up. Keep going, Raine, and you'll be on the other side."

The other side was like standing in the sky. A place so high I could see the whole of Sparrow Road—the artists' sheds, our cottage, the path to Sorrow Lake, the old gray barn we'd wandered past this morning, the ancient glassy greenhouse, the turtle pond, another bench swing underneath a gnarled oak. And tucked back in the woods, an old white building Viktor hadn't shown us on our tour.

"What's that?" I asked when Diego finally stood beside me on the deck.

"That's the old infirmary. The place the orphans went when they were sick. The Iceberg lives there now."

"The infirmary? Do you think Viktor has a phone?"

"A phone?" Diego looked surprised. "I would imagine that he does. You got a call to make?"

"I might," I said.

"Not me," Diego said. "At home, I'm so busy teaching college I'm glad to have it gone. All of it. Telephones, TVs. Newspapers. Radio. Nothing but pure peace."

"You are?" I groaned. Diego seemed too happy to like the Iceberg's rules.

"Time floats at Sparrow Road." Diego smiled. "There's nothing here to mark the days but sun. I don't even keep a calendar. For all I know it's January now."

I laughed. "It's July seventh."

"It is?" Diego looked surprised. "Oh, right. We just saw the fireworks in Comfort!"

"But the silence until supper?" I asked. "Every day? That sounds absolutely horrible."

"I know." Diego nodded. "It sounds bad in the beginning. But trust me, you'll learn to like it, Raine. If Josie can keep quiet, anybody can." He laughed and leaned his elbows on the railing. "And Sparrow Road's the perfect place for dreams."

"Dreams?"

"Sure. Like the way you start to daydream when you're bored. Or, there's nothing but the quiet, so you dream."

I thought of sixth-grade science and how Mr. Wetmore's lectures on amoebas always made me daydream. But I wouldn't want to do that every day. "Six days a week till supper? That's a lot of bored."

"Oh, it's not boring really. Because an artist just gets busy and creates. All that time alone becomes a painting or a poem. Josie fills her quiet up with quilts."

"When I was young I used to dream up stories," I said. "But that won't keep me busy until supper."

Diego laughed again. "You're still young, Raine. And you might be surprised how much you create in all the quiet. You could write a book at Sparrow Road."

"About what?" I said.

"Who knows?" Diego smiled. "That's part of the discovery. Just start out on a journey. Ask yourself, What if? Or think about what was or what could be. And suddenly"—he snapped his fingers—"like magic, you'll be drifting in a dream."

"What if?" I asked. *"What was? Or what could be?"* Diego made the silence sound enchanted. Not a rule, but a chance.

"I swear it works for me," Diego said. "Just give a try tomorrow. Let me know what you dream up."

I'm going off to write, I wrote to Mama the next morning. I was eager to drift off in the daydream Diego promised was ahead.

"Write?" Mama glanced up from her Betty Crocker cookbook.

I shook my head and pressed my finger to my lips. *The rule,* I wrote. I wanted to spend one full day in silence, the way the artists did, so I could see if what Diego said was true.

Mama looked at me, confused. She didn't know about my tour of the tower, or the attic, or the games of Old Maid I played with Lillian. She only knew I met two artists when I wandered from the cottage. A thing she said I shouldn't have done, but she was too troubled after town to ask me questions, too lost in thought like she had something weighing heavy on her mind.

We can talk here in the cottage, Mama wrote.

I'm going to try the silence until supper.

Why??? Why'd you change your mind? Mama studied me like she was staring at a stranger.

I shrugged. This was already too much talk. I wanted to get out in the meadow, the place Diego said a dream would surely come. I zipped my backpack closed. I'd packed two pens, a box of colored pencils, and a sketchbook Diego gave me for my dreams.

OK, Mama wrote. She scrunched her worried eyebrows. *But stay where I can see you.*

I will. I'd spent my life so close to Grandpa Mac and Mama, I never had the nerve to wander far.

Outside in the meadow, I stood still for a second. Diego was right. Sparrow Road wasn't really silent. It was filled with a background hum most people didn't slow down long enough to hear. A steady insect buzz, birdsong, the rustle of leaf brushing against leaf. I could even hear the wind whistle through the weeds. If I stood still long enough, Diego said, I might just hear the sun.

I crossed the grass and settled on a bench beneath a weeping willow.

Sparrow Road, I wrote down in my sketchbook. *Who left that breakfast basket at our door? Why did Mama bring us here for the last half of my summer?* Diego said most daydreams started with a question, a wonder, a puzzle you couldn't solve. A blank space for the imagination to create. *What was wrong with Mama when she came back from town? Why didn't she take me with her?*

A red dragonfly landed on my leg. Doves cooed in the

distance. I couldn't believe my kind of wonders could ever fill a day.

What if? I wrote. Wasn't that all Diego said I'd need to get a story started?

What if ghosts really lived up in that attic?

What if the orphans were still here?

What if I was an orphan?

I stopped and stared out at the hills. If Mama died today, I would be an orphan, a girl without any parents left. Only I wouldn't end up in an orphanage like the kids at Sparrow Road; I'd have Grandpa Mac.

But what if Grandpa Mac got really old? Like Lillian? Or what if he died suddenly? Who would take me then? Would I go to an orphanage?

All of my what-ifs seemed more like worries than a dream. It was thoughts like these that made me hate to sit in silence by myself. The kind of what-ifs that sometimes made me anxious before I fell asleep. I tore the questions from my sketchbook and started a fresh page. I didn't want to imagine Grandpa Mac or Mama gone.

What was? I wrote. *What was or what could be?*

Who were those orphans who lived up in the attic?

Who owned those small toys buried in the dust?

Who drew those faded drawings?

A cardinal settled on a low branch, flicked its wings, and waited. I closed my eyes. Maybe daydreams came faster in the dark.

Once I had a family, someone said. *People think we didn't have parents. We had parents. Everybody does. They had to be there once upon a time.*

It was a boy's voice I imagined, a boy's voice speaking in my daydream. A story, just like Diego promised. A boy I'd never seen, but there he was. In old wool pants that hung below his knees, scuffed ankle boots, a flannel shirt rolled up at the sleeves. A boy who lived up in that attic. His skinny lower legs were nicked and scarred. His face was round, his eyes the same grassy green as Mama's.

Life just has a way, he said. *I think you must know what I mean. Even parents can get lost.*

I opened up my eyes and wrote it down in one mad rush. Everything he told me. Word after word. I wrote so long a red writer's bump rose up on my finger. One morning in the silence and the dream Diego promised had already arrived.

"It worked!" I told Diego. At five o'clock he'd come into the main house to help Mama with the supper. Lillian too. I stood beside him cutting Mama's carrots. Lillian sliced mushrooms. Mama didn't want the artists to help her in the kitchen, but no matter how many ways she said it, they still refused to leave. I could tell both of them were trying to welcome Mama, the same way they welcomed me.

"What worked?" Mama stopped her stirring. The smell of melted cheese and garlic drifted from her pot.

"What was or what could be?" I said to Diego. "I tried it and my imagination went to work."

"You make it the whole day without a word?" Diego winked, like he already knew I didn't.

"Not quite," I said. By lunch, Mama and I were chatting in our cottage, but when she asked about my writing, I kept the orphan to myself.

"What was or what could be?" Mama interrupted.

"Is that what you were doing underneath that willow? Thinking of what was?"

"Sort of." I didn't want to explain it all to Mama; it was Diego I wanted most to tell. Diego, who knew how daydreams worked. I wished she'd go back to her cooking and let me talk to Diego by myself.

"I don't think Raine's imagination needs any help," Mama said, concerned. "It already runs wild."

"Oh, it's really nothing, Molly," Diego said, embarrassed. I could see that he was struck by Mama's beauty—her mane of copper curls, her bright green eyes. Lots of men liked Mama, but Mama never had the time to like them back. "It's just a thing I mentioned yesterday to Raine. While you were in town shopping. How we artists make it through the silence with our dreams." He snuck another wink my way; I was glad he left out the part about the tower.

"Yesterday," Mama scolded, "Raine shouldn't have left the cottage. I hope she didn't disturb your work."

"Not at all," Diego said.

"The children must be hungry." Lillian looked at me like I was lost behind some fog. "They always need to eat."

"Well, I certainly am hungry!" a woman bellowed.

"Josie!" Lillian clapped her tiny hands.

Suddenly Josie marched into the kitchen, her long, sure steps reminding me of the cowboys in the westerns Grandpa watched. Except in place of cowboy boots, she had on men's black work boots, big and clunky, with heavy silver buckles that jangled when she walked. Her dress looked like a patchwork sack of scraps. A nest of neon braids framed her freckled face.

"You've come home!" Lillian said.

"I'll always come home, Lilly." Josie smacked a kiss on Lillian's head. "Oh boy," she said. "I'm beat. Two days of watching clouds drift really wore me out." She gave a great big laugh.

"We have a brand-new orphan," Lillian said.

"Fabulous," Josie cheered. "We need more orphans at this place." A wide gap flashed between her two front teeth. She gave my hand a forceful shake. "So you must be the long-awaited Raine O'Rourke."

"I am," I said, although no one ever called me long awaited.

"And that means you must be Molly." Josie latched on to Mama's hand and shook it hard. She towered at least two heads above Mama and she was sturdy as a tree. "I hear you took my job." She slapped Mama on the shoulder.

"At last!" Diego laughed. "No more of your horrible carrot stew! These two came to our rescue from Milwaukee."

"Milwaukee?" Josie whistled. "My oh my! How did Viktor find you in Milwaukee?"

"He just did," Mama said abruptly. She waved the steam back from her face. Red fluster blotches rose up

39

on her neck. "Right now I need to get this dinner served. So if the three of you could gather at the table— "

"Not served," Josie said. She pulled a stack of plates out of the cupboard. "All of us will help."

"Not anymore," Mama said. "Viktor hired me. And please don't put down plates for us."

"No plates for you and Raine?" Diego frowned.

"The two of us will eat here in the kitchen." Mama sounded like a servant. "After your meal has been served."

"What?" I said. "We can't eat dinner now?" Warm garlic bread was waiting in the oven. I'd been craving Mama's tortellini since this morning. It was her specialty, the birthday meal Grandpa Mac requested every year.

"You eat with us or no one eats," Josie ordered.

"Ladies, you heard Josie," Diego said. "And you can see," he joked, "I can't afford to starve."

Eleanor didn't want us at the table and everybody saw it the second she sat down. "I see we have a crowd tonight," she sniffed. In her straight black skirt and ruffled blouse she looked too formal to be here for Mama's supper.

"Let me introduce—" Diego waved his fork in our direction.

"I know who they are," Eleanor said.

"Raine and Molly," Josie finished off the sentence. She yanked a hunk of warm bread from the loaf and dropped it on my plate.

"So Viktor won't be joining us for dinner?" Mama's hands were folded in her lap like she wasn't going to eat.

"Never," Josie said. "The Iceberg eats alone."

"The Iceberg?" Mama said. "That isn't very nice." Mama hated mean names—even when they fit.

"It certainly is not," Eleanor said. She snapped her napkin open; it was the same embroidered pattern someone had stitched for us. The towered house. The initials sewn in the corner. I looked around the table. There was one at every plate.

Josie nudged me with her elbow. "I sewed two sets, so you'll have one at your cottage and one here in the main house." The painted eggs, the tangerines, the golden glittered WELCOME. It *was* lively Josie who left that basket at our door.

"Thanks," I said. "They're beautiful. I'll save one as a keepsake."

"Well, they're impractical for meals," Eleanor said. "But charming, I suppose. Josie seems to have the time for crafts."

"This is our summer orphan," Lillian said.

"She's not an orphan," Eleanor corrected. "She's the daughter of the maid. There are no orphans here. This is an artists' retreat." She shifted in her chair but she wouldn't look at me. "I shall assume tonight is an exception. I hadn't planned to have a child at the meal. I understood this summer would be spent among adults. Otherwise, my daughters could be here."

"You have kids?" I blurted. I couldn't picture someone as stiff as Eleanor with children.

"Eleanor has three young daughters," Josie said. "All home with a nanny while she writes."

"My husband's in Chicago with the children." Eleanor

stabbed a piece of lettuce with her fork. She hadn't even tasted Mama's food.

"You left them for the summer?" I thought of how mad I was yesterday when Mama went to town. Except for work and school, and sleepovers I sometimes had with friends, the two of us hardly were apart. "Would you ever do that, Mama?"

"No," Mama said. "I couldn't."

"Well, I have work that must be done without my daughters," Eleanor said to me. "Not everyone can be a maid."

"Mama is a singer." I don't know why I said it. Mama hadn't really sung since I was little, not much more than lullabies or hymns. But once she did. I wanted Eleanor to know Mama was more than just a maid. More than a waitress. More than a summer cook. "Mama had a music scholarship to college."

"You sing?" Diego grinned.

Mama's face burned pink. "I sang."

"In Amsterdam," I added. I always thought Amsterdam made Mama's singing sound important, even if she was just a young girl hippie singing on the street. A life I'd only seen in pictures. The boat where I was born. Me, a barefoot toddler twirling on the street. Mama with a guitar on her shoulder.

"Wow!" Diego said. "Amsterdam? How long ago was that?"

"Another life." Mama blew a frizzy curl back from her face. Beads of sweat glistened on her forehead. "When Raine was very young."

"A singer? How impressive," Eleanor mocked. "So did you perform professionally?"

"No," Mama said, "I didn't."

"Ah," Eleanor said. "So it really was a hobby?"

Mama shoved her chair back from the table. "May I get anybody anything?" I knew she was going to the kitchen to scream into a towel. It was her waitress trick when she had a cranky customer.

Diego reached for Mama's chair. "Molly, please don't wait on us. Sit down and eat."

"No," Mama said. "I've already had enough."

After that bad meal, Mama made us eat every supper by ourselves, alone in the big kitchen, with milk in crystal goblets and china plates and Josie's hand-stitched napkins spread out on our laps. Mama tried her best to make it seem like she wasn't just a servant. "It's no different from my job at Christos," she said whenever I complained. "I can't sit with my customers." But the artists weren't our customers. Already that first week everyone but Eleanor treated us as friends. And it was the artists I wanted to sit beside at supper.

Still, every night at five o'clock Diego, Lillian, and Josie gathered in the kitchen to dice and cut and mash and mix. While we worked, the room filled up with stories. Josie told about the troubled teens she taught art to in Detroit, and Diego talked about his sons when they were young. The pranks they played. He said both his boys were grown up and gone, and that his wife, Sophia, died too early, so now he lived in California all alone. Lillian talked about the orphans or Viktor as a prodigy, her piano students, the

St. Paul seniors' high-rise that she hated. Sometimes I told a story from Milwaukee, but mostly I just listened, the way I did to all the folks who shopped at Grandpa's store.

Mornings, while Mama planted flowers or hung laundry on the line, she let me wander Sparrow Road alone as long as I stayed near the main house or the cottage. Sometimes, when I was sure no one was watching, I'd sneak up the servants' staircase, drag a chair over to the ladder, and climb up to the tower by myself. Of all the spots at Sparrow Road, the tower was my favorite place to dream.

From my spy perch in the sky, I could see Viktor strolling slouch-shouldered through the meadow or napping on a hammock in the shade. The Iceberg. He still hadn't said a single word to me, not even a thank-you on those nights Mama made me deliver supper to his door. A job I hated, but Mama made me do it.

Other times, I spied Mama on the path to the infirmary, Viktor's house and office, a place Josie said the artists wouldn't be welcome, but it seemed to me Mama always was. Something about the two of them still struck me as too friendly. Except for Lillian, Mama was the only person Viktor gave more than a nod.

I sat down with my back against the tower. The little plywood lap desk Diego built me was propped up on my legs. I'd found it in the tower with a note that said, *Sweet dreams. D.* I pulled my sketchbook from my backpack and found an empty page.

Through the trees, I could hear the faint stop and start of Viktor's cello. Only it wasn't music really. Viktor's music sounded more like suffering than songs. Whines and cries and shrieks. A playground fight. The howl of children hurt. Other times, there was the clang of his piano or the whine of a violin. Diego said Viktor's dreadful music didn't break the silence rule because music was his art. And besides, he composed in the infirmary with all the windows shut. Far enough away that the artists couldn't hear it in their sheds.

Why does all his music sound so sad? I wrote down in my sketchbook. *Why does he drink tea with Lillian at night on the side porch? Why does Mama go to the infirmary so often? If Viktor was a prodigy, how did he end up here?*

I flipped the page; I didn't want to daydream about Viktor.

What was? I wrote to get my dreaming started. *What was or what could be?*

Your days, I wrote. *Did you have to sit in silence just like me?* Often if I asked a question, my orphan's story would get started.

I closed my eyes and pictured his mop of thick brown hair, his chipped front tooth, the scar across his eyebrow. The more days I imagined him, the more alive he seemed to be. Real, the way people were in books.

My days, he finally said. *They were like everybody else's. We were quiet during classes. At dinner during prayer. In summer we*

played baseball right there in the meadow. There were so many of us
kids, we made up our own teams.

Everyone is gone, I wrote. Your orphanage is closed.

Closed? he asked. Did the orphans all find families?

I don't know, I wrote. I wonder that myself.

"Do you think they all found families?" I asked Josie. Most
nights, after we'd dried the final dishes, Josie and I liked to
take a nightly sojourn to the attic. Nightly sojourn, that's
what Josie always called it. The attic was the only place I
ever saw her still, her voice dropped to a whisper like we
were visiting a church.

"I don't know." Josie shook her head. Even calm, she
looked too wild for the attic. Every dress she wore was
made from colored scraps of fabric stitched together, rainbow clothes as lively as her braids. "But I'd sure like to
find out."

"Me too," I said. "It's like their time here ended in mid-
stream. Suddenly." I looked around the room at the tiny
toys and trinkets. The emerald rosary hanging from the
bed. Yellowed sheets of cursive work like I did back in
third grade. "It feels like the orphans wanted us to find it
all and wonder. To think about their days. The way things
used to be."

"Yeah, I see that," Josie said. "And for some reason,
Viktor let it be. Left all of it untouched."

I walked over to a drawing. It was a chalky sketch of snowy hills colored on black paper, Sparrow Road in winter. The neighbors' small red barn set far off in the distance. The white hills so cold and empty, I could almost feel the chill.

I stared hard at the bottom of the paper. There, in faded pencil, someone had printed LYMAN CHASE. And under that AGE 12.

Lyman, I said inside my heart where my orphan always heard me. So far no one knew his story, even Josie; I was happiest to keep my daydreams to myself. *Lyman Chase. I finally know your name.*

Yep, he said. *I've been Lyman all along.*

12

"Raine." Lillian's weak voice shocked me from my daydream. From the swing on the front porch, I'd been imagining the orphans building snowmen in the winter. Coming in for oatmeal. Warming their cold hands around the fire in the parlor. A chapter in my story I still wanted to write.

"Shh." I put my finger to my lips. Even though Mama and Viktor had gone to town again, and Josie and Diego were working in their sheds, Eleanor was here. From an open upstairs window I could hear the constant click of typing. If I could hear her, she could hear us, too.

"I just need some company," Lillian said, like she was sad. "Would you read to me, dear child?"

I shook my head no. Josie said the silence rule was serious—one violation and the artist had to leave. I didn't want Lillian sent back to that high-rise in St. Paul.

"Please," Lillian begged. "Just a page or two. I have a poem book all picked out."

I held my sketchbook up to show that I was writing. If Eleanor heard us talking on the front porch, she would be the first to tell.

"Please?" Lillian asked again. "I can't sit in this silence for so long. It makes me miss the children. I don't know where they've gone."

Saying no to Lillian was too hard for my heart. She always made me think of Grandpa Mac—how he'd feel if he were frail and made to sit in silence by himself. A thing he couldn't bear. If he begged someone for their company, I'd want them to say yes.

Okay, I finally motioned with a shrug. We could do it in the library. I'd close both doors and whisper. And hope we didn't get caught.

It was late that night when Viktor stood outside our cottage. The second that I saw him a wave of guilt rose up in my chest.

"Viktor," Mama said, surprised. He hadn't visited our cottage in the ten days since we came. "Come in."

"No, thank you, Molly." He stared down at his feet. "I'd like a word with Raine."

A sour knot twisted in my stomach.

"Raine?" Mama asked. "Viktor, is there something wrong?"

I walked out the front door before he had a chance to answer. I broke the silence rule. I knew why he was here.

"The silence." Viktor's bony hands were hidden in his pocket. "We keep it for good reason."

"I know." I'd already learned how silence worked on dreams, how my orphan's story came alive because of quiet.

"And the artists have committed to a contract. But Lillian—" He rubbed his hand over his sunken cheek. Even in the darkness, the Iceberg's skin was the blue white of a ghost.

"The silence made her sad," I said. "Please don't make her go back to that high-rise in St. Paul."

"That high-rise?" Viktor said. "What a dismal place." He stared down at the grass. "Lillian, she finds the silence long. Perhaps if you could sit with her each day? Help her write her poetry?"

"Help her write?" For some reason, I wasn't sure Lillian really was a poet. Maybe because I'd never seen her write. "During silent time?" Was Viktor asking me to break one of his rules?

"Yes," Viktor said. "So she's not alone so long. Each afternoon, the two of you may have the side porch to yourselves. Close the door so no one hears you. I will inform the other artists an exception has been made." This was more talk than I'd ever heard from Viktor. I felt like I was drowning in a sudden flood of words. Still, he kept his focus on the ground.

"I shall pay you for your time."

"No." Grandpa Mac didn't pay me for working in his store. It was family helping family. And Lillian already felt like a kind of family. A great-great-aunt or the grandma I didn't have.

"I would prefer," he said.

"No," I said again. "I don't want the money." I was glad to have a job to fill my days. Like Lillian, I couldn't stand the silence for too long.

"Good night, then." He took a step and turned to look at me. "After everything she's given—" He stopped like he couldn't quite find the words. "It's fitting that a child be kind to her."

13

"Mama, what's in Comfort?" I asked her the next day.

We were stretched out on a blanket at the lake with a picnic lunch of ham sandwiches, ripple chips, and pickles.

"Stores and things." Mama flushed. "Nothing really, Raine."

"And you go there to buy groceries?" Both times Mama had gone to town with Viktor she'd brushed her curls, put on clean clothes and earrings like there was more to Comfort than shopping for our food. And both times she'd come back with fluster blotches burning on her neck.

"I do," Mama said. "Why the questions, Raine? You've seen the bags yourself. You've helped unload the groceries."

"I know." I had, but there was something suspicious about her trips to town with Viktor. Like her sudden summer job at Sparrow Road, Mama's answers didn't add up. No matter how many times I asked. "But why can't you take me with you into town? And why'd we move here in the first place?"

"For heaven's sake, Raine!" Mama forced a little laugh. "I thought we put this all to rest. It's a summer in the country. And I'm working, Raine. Every day but Sunday. Cooking, cleaning. Earning money."

"I know," I said. I didn't want Mama to get mad. "But why won't you take me into town?"

"I will." Mama looked up at the sky. Two sheep clouds and a palm tree floated past, but Mama didn't see them. She didn't have Josie's gift for finding pictures in the clouds.

"Or I can go with Josie and Diego. They bike in all the time. And Diego found an old bike in the barn; one he said would fit me. He's fixing up the chain. Lowering the seat."

"No," Mama answered quickly. "I'll take you in with me." She brushed a strand of hair back from my face. "We haven't even been at Sparrow Road two weeks. Isn't there enough here to explore? You're always in a hurry to discover something new. Uncover the next thing."

"Not a hurry," I said. "I just want to bike to Comfort. See more than Sparrow Road."

"I thought you liked it here. The artists. The way you get to roam around the grounds. That writing that you do. You seem happier each day. Not so homesick for Milwaukee. Or TV." Mama tried to joke. She was glad to have the TV gone.

"I still miss TV," I said, "and Grandpa Mac and Beauty."

I did, but every day my homesick faded some. I'd already written Grandpa Mac three letters, one more than he had written me. And once Mama let me call from the infirmary, alone, while she waited outside on a bench.

"The quiet will be over soon enough," Mama said. "For now, let's just enjoy the peace."

"I do. But I still want to bike to town. See the things I'm missing. Josie says there are root beer floats, and pies, and turtle sundaes, and lemon bars, and a five-and-dime where we can trinket shop."

"Ah, Raine." Mama's voice was weary. "You're always missing something. Or imagining what's missing."

"That isn't true," I said. "Not always."

"It is." Mama shook her head. "And you've been that way since the beginning. A wonderer. I think that's why you and Josie spend so much time up in that attic. So you can think about what's missing. All those mysteries you dream up in your mind." Mama said that last part like I was doing something wrong.

"I don't know." I took a bite of dry ham sandwich; in all the heat the bread had turned to toast. "Maybe so," I finally said.

I was a girl born with something missing. *Someone* missing, but I wasn't going to say it. I'd learned long ago he was someone Mama wanted gone.

Do you think about what's missing?
I wrote Lyman.

Missing? Lyman leaned against the railing of the tower.

You know, I wrote. *People. Like your parents?*

Sure, he said. *I wonder where they went. Why they couldn't keep me. Anybody would.* He pulled a paper airplane from his pocket and launched it on a slow drift with the breeze. *We all think about what's missing. And when someone's gone, we have to dream them up. Same way you dream up me.*

What about your dad? I said.

Gone. We watched his paper airplane glide down to the grass. *Same as yours, I guess.*

"Were you close to your father?" I asked Lillian. We were reading Robert Frost out on the side porch, Lillian rocking in her Dream Chair, a gift Josie found at a garage sale in Comfort and painted with pink stars. Josie promised Lillian that when September came, she'd find a way to get the Dream Chair to St. Paul.

"My father?" Lillian blinked. Mama said it was cataracts that made Lillian's pupils milky.

I stuck my finger in the page and closed the dusty book. I was ready for a rest; my tongue was tired of tripping over words. Line by line, the poems were like a long walk through the darkness. My brain was worn out.

"Yes," I said. "Your father. You never mention him." In all her stories, Lillian never said a word about her family.

"No." Lillian shook her head. "I'm afraid that I didn't know him."

"Never?"

"No." Lillian frowned.

"I don't know mine either." Through the corner of my eye I spied Eleanor skulking past the side porch.

"Her," Lillian said when Eleanor huffed off. "I don't think she should be working with the children. The children need more love."

"She's not with the children," I said. "Her children are at home."

"She's a mother?" Lillian gasped. "How terrible. My mother was so sweet."

"Mine too," I said. "I mean my mother is."

Lillian patted at my leg. "I'm sure you miss her, dear." No matter how many times I told her, Lillian couldn't remember who Mama really was.

"So you knew your mother then?" I asked.

"Oh yes," Lillian said. "Mother was a saint. The day she brought me here, they gave us each a sausage. And Mother gave me hers, because she knew that I was hungry." Lillian's hazy eyes filled up with tears. "Afterward, I was so sorry that I ate it, I threw up in the snow."

"The snow?"

"We came here in the winter. So many children did. Families who couldn't survive out in the cold. But the mothers couldn't stay. Fathers either. They only kept the children, so Mother had to say good-bye."

"So were you an orphan, Lillian?" For the first time since I met her, Lillian's story was starting to make sense. Once she was an orphan in this house. "Did you live up in the attic?"

"Oh no," Lillian pressed her palm against her chest. "The attic was for boys."

15

"I think Lillian was an orphan," I told
Josie. I sank the oars deep in the water and tried to row the
old boat forward. Teaching me to row was one of Josie's
missions. *Independence*, she told Mama. *Raine needs it to be
ready for the world.*

"An orphan? I had her figured for a teacher," Josie said.
"All that talk of spelling and piano."

"I know," I said. "But maybe she was both."

Lillian was another mystery we both wanted to solve.
Her odd friendship with Viktor, her talk about the children, all her mixed-up memories. Neither of us knew what
in all of that was real.

"Today she said she came here in the winter with her
mother. And her mother had to leave, because the parents
couldn't stay. They only kept the kids."

"I think that part is true enough," Josie said. "Folks
in town have told me. They said sometimes they'd spot a
threadbare mom or dad walking brokenhearted down the
road. Even in the winter."

"They told you that in town? Who?"

"Oh, just friends I've made in Comfort. Folks I chat with in the shops. The café. When I'm tired of the quiet, I bike to town to talk. Viktor can't enforce the silence rule there!"

"Have you seen Mama there with Viktor?" Maybe Josie knew what Mama did in town.

"Can't say I have," Josie said. "But I don't go there to buy groceries. I'm happy to eat the feasts your mama makes. Why you asking, Raine?"

"I don't know. I guess the trips she makes to Comfort seem a little strange. Like the way she took this job so suddenly? One day we were living in Milwaukee, and the next day we were gone."

"I suppose it's strange to take a job that quickly," Josie said. "But you know me, sometimes I also move too fast. And anyway, I'm glad your mama did. I can't imagine this summer without you. Or food!" Josie grabbed the oars and steered us from the weeds. "Almost hit a snag."

"Maybe if I saw Comfort for myself?" I said. "Went to town with you?"

"Absolutely!" Josie cheered. "A new adventure is ahead!" In the final blaze of sunset, her neon braids glowed cotton candy pink. "We'll get to make a memory!" Every day Josie sewed a brand-new patch of memory so in the end her summer would be a kind of quilt. "Root beer floats at the Comfort Cone. Marge's lemon bars at the sweet Blue Moon Café. How soon can we set out?"

"Tomorrow?"

"Tomorrow would be perfect! We ought to take a practice run the day before the Rhubarb Social. Eight miles into town might feel long the first time." The Rhubarb Social at Good Shepherd was Josie's latest scheme. She insisted everyone would go this weekend. Everyone but Eleanor. Mama and Lillian would ride in Viktor's truck. I'd bike in with Josie and Diego.

"Tomorrow then," I said.

"I hope your mama lets you, Raine. I know she keeps you close."

"She will," I lied. I wasn't going to ask Mama until the minute I was leaving, until I had Josie's power right beside me, so Mama would say yes.

"Take a look at that!" Josie said. Out in the water, Mama and Diego floated like driftwood on their backs. Mama lifted up her hand and gave a little wave. "You think those two are a mystery?"

"Nope," I said. It seemed most evenings Diego stayed by Mama. Washing dishes. Talking on the swing. Bringing ice cream to our cottage. Sunset swims with us when Mama would say yes. "Diego definitely likes her."

"You bet he does. But I'd say he likes you both."

By the time we all got back to the house, lanterns burned along the side porch, and through the screen I could see the silhouettes of Lillian and Viktor.

"What about a fire?" Diego set his hand on Mama's back, but Mama stepped away.

"Yes!" I said. The only fires in Milwaukee were emergencies.

"Hey, you two," Josie shouted to Lillian and Viktor. "S'mores. Marshmallows and chocolate bars on me."

"Oh yes," Lillian said. "A roasted marshmallow would be lovely."

"If you'd like," Viktor said to Lillian.

"A miracle!" Josie pinched my waist. "The Iceberg's going to join us, Raine! Maybe Eleanor will be next?"

"Oh no!" I said. "She would ruin it all."

Eleanor didn't come down to the fire, but it was strange enough to have Viktor in our circle. He didn't say a single word; he just roasted marshmallows for Lillian and slid them on a plate.

In the fire glow everyone looked happy—even Viktor, whose hollow face seemed to brighten through the flames. I licked the sticky marshmallow off my fingers, breathed in the smell of burning wood.

"Tonight the children will sleep down at the water," Lillian said. "I'm afraid the attic is too hot."

"We'll see," Viktor said, as though the children were still here.

"What we need at this fire is some music," Josie said. "Someone who can sing and play guitar!"

"Molly does," Viktor said. "She both sings and plays guitar." How did Viktor know Mama played guitar? Mama hadn't played it since we moved back to Milwaukee; she always said her music days were done in Amsterdam.

"Guitar?" Diego smiled. "Another talent, Molly?"

Mama slouched down in her lawn chair. "I really don't do either."

"Ah, Molly." Viktor looked at Mama as if they shared a secret. "I am certain that you do."

"So how does Viktor know you played guitar?" I grabbed a damp towel from the basket and pinned it on the line. I'd volunteered to help Mama hang the laundry, so she'd be in good spirits when Josie came to take me into town.

Mama looked up toward the house, then pulled the clothespin from her teeth. "Shush," she whispered.

"We're far enough away," I said. "Eleanor won't hear. And Viktor's gone. And Josie and Diego are working in their sheds."

Mama shook her head, then handed me a soggy sheet.

"Did you tell Viktor?" I asked. Mama never talked about those years she was a singer. Her hippie years in Amsterdam were like a thing that never happened. A crazy Mama-phase Grandpa Mac said was better left forgotten.

Mama shrugged like she couldn't quite remember.

"But he knew you played guitar?" That part surprised me most of all. Guitar was Mama's hidden talent. Even I had never heard her play it—except maybe as a baby, and I couldn't remember that.

Mama took one end of the sheet, stretched it on the line, and pinned it tight. She wasn't going to talk.

"Did you know him back in Amsterdam?"

Mama's eyes grew huge. *No.* She crinkled up her face like my question was pure crazy.

Then, before I could ask Mama another string of questions, Josie came strolling through the meadow, balancing a bike with each big hand. Just as we had planned. One for her and one for me.

Mama looked confused.

"Town," I said. "I'm going in with Josie."

No! This time Mama shook her head like she really, really meant it.

When Josie made it all the way to us, she passed the red bike off to me. It was old, with rusted fenders and fat tires, but it was good enough to get me into Comfort.

Josie opened up her hands. *Root beer floats* was printed on one palm. *The great escape* was written on the other.

No, Mama shook her head again.

Josie looked confused. She cocked her head like she needed Mama to explain. Then she took a pen out of her pocket. *It's town,* she wrote on her arm. *We aren't going far.*

No, Mama mouthed. She grabbed the pen and wrote across her hand. *I'm going to take Raine to town with me.*

"I want to go with Josie," I said. I didn't care about the silence rule, but I knew Josie wouldn't break it. Mama either. And it was easier to argue with Mama when I knew she wouldn't speak. "We're going for a memory," I said.

Raine is safe with me, Josie wrote in giant letters on the inside of my arm.

"I am," I said.

Mama huffed a long, slow sigh, the kind of sound she made when she was mad. Then she grabbed me by the shoulders, her laundry hands still damp, and whispered in my ear, "Don't talk to any strangers." She said it like we were right back in Milwaukee, like I was walking to the library alone.

"I won't." I pulled away. I didn't want Mama's worries to ruin something fun.

"I mean it, Raine," she whispered. "Not a single soul."

By the time we got to Comfort, I was so tired, I staggered when I stood. Eight miles was a long ride for a sleepy, main street town.

"You look like you just climbed down from a horse," Josie joked. She dropped her heavy arm over my shoulder. "Come on, partner, the root beer float's on me."

We left the bikes, unlocked, against the five-and-dime. Comfort wasn't much more than a few brick shops, a couple old cafés. Shady blocks of tidy houses. A small white church perched up on a hill. A safety Mama would have seen during her trips to town with Viktor. As far as I could tell there wasn't any danger, no reason Mama had to keep me from this town.

"Comfort Cone, here we come!" Josie shouted. She flung her arms wide open to the world; the few people on the street gave us a stare. "First root beer floats, then the Blue Moon Café for Marge's lemon bars." Josie grinned. "Trinket shopping at the five-and-dime." She rubbed her giant hand against my head. "One of these days," she said, "your mama's going to have to let you go."

"I know," I said. "And Grandpa Mac is worse! You should have seen them in Milwaukee. They always say it's because I'm an only child. Mama says it's easier to worry over one."

"Could be," Josie said. "If you were mine, I guess I'd keep you close. But even so, you need to know the world!"

Comfort wasn't quite the world, but still I was happy that we came. On our short walk down the street Josie gave a wave or nod to everyone we passed. "Great day!" she'd say, as if every staring stranger was her friend. "There it is!" She pointed toward a rundown shack with a plastic statue of a twist cone stuck up on the roof. Faded picnic tables were scattered out in front. "The Comfort Cone at last!"

When we reached the little window, a burly bald man slid the small screen open for our order. "This is Dave," Josie said to me. "He's the owner of this ice cream palace. And that handsome boy is Leif, Dave's son." Leif was curly haired and cute, not much older than me; it embarrassed me to have Josie call him handsome.

"And gentlemen"—Josie shoved me forward—"this would be Raine O'Rourke. One of our summer writers." Heat burned under my cheeks.

"A writer? You hear that, Leif?" Dave said. "This girl here can write."

"No." I blushed. "Not really." Now I knew how Mama felt when Viktor said she was a singer. It seemed too big to call myself a writer.

"Well, you sure have a pool of talent at that place!" Dave said. "And how's that patchwork quilt today?"

"Under construction," Josie said. "It's why Raine biked with me to town. We're here to make a memory. Today's square will be a root beer float in honor of the Comfort Cone and my first trip to town with Raine."

"Sounds good by me." Dave didn't seem bothered by Josie's wild braids or her floppy patchwork dress or her big black boots with buckles. He didn't stare like the people who passed us on the street. "Two then, Leif," he called. Behind him, Leif began to mix our floats. "So how's life at Sparrow Road?"

"Great!" Josie said. "Right now we're planning our first festival. An arts festival. So the town can come out to see the work we've done this summer. The Sparrow Road Arts Extravaganza! It'll be a giant bash where all the guests make art."

"What?" I said. "A party at Sparrow Road?" Josie's sudden scheme was news to me; every day another wild idea popped into Josie's brain, but this one was the wildest of all. Viktor would never let her throw a party at the house.

Josie gave my neck a sweaty squeeze. "Yep! I've been inspired by the Rhubarb Social tomorrow at Good Shepherd. I figured if Comfort could host a shindig, we could throw one, too." She propped her hands against her hips. "Gatherings are good."

"A gathering out there might change the way folks see it. The dark cloud over that place," Dave said. "Most people still think of it as a place for misfit kids, even though they left there years ago."

"Not necessarily misfits," Josie said. "Just kids without a home."

"True enough." Dave slid the root beer floats to Josie. "Two dollars ought to do it."

Josie handed him her money and then plopped a dollop of soft vanilla ice cream on her tongue. "Mmm-mmm, heaven," she hummed. "And you'll come to see my quilt. The memory square I stitch for Comfort Cone." She knocked her knuckles twice against the wooden counter. "Be well," she said. "Peace. And Leif, Dave. Don't forget the Arts Extravaganza!"

"Sure thing." Dave slid the tiny screen door shut. "But don't count on me for making any art."

"You never know." Josie took a big slurp of the root beer. "You might surprise yourself."

"Arts Extravaganza?" I asked Josie. "You're kidding, right?"

She hiked her patchwork dress up to her knees and straddled the splintered picnic table bench. "I was just trying out that name. We can call it something else. Oh, look!" She dug an Orange Crush cap out of the dirt and dropped it in her bag. "A treasure for Diego!" Diego liked to think of trash as treasure—nuts and bolts, lost keys, a broken bird egg we found once on a walk—all of it he put into his art. So Josie kept her eye out for good trash.

"Viktor won't let us have a party," I said.

"Why not? A party's a great thing!" She lifted her bright face up to the sun. "And besides, maybe the orphans would come home."

"The orphans?" What did Josie mean? The orphans would be grown up by now. And Lyman wouldn't be the boy that I imagined. I wanted him to stay the orphan in my dreams. "How would you ever find them?"

"I don't know yet." Josie stretched her legs out on the bench. "But I bet you that we could."

I sucked the sweet bubbles through my straw. "I thought Viktor wanted to forget about the orphans. Old ghosts, Diego said. It's why Viktor keeps the attic locked."

"Maybe so," Josie said. "But don't you think the past is better faced? Even if it's sad? Sometimes trying to forget isn't worth the trouble."

"But Viktor will never let—"

"Speaking of—," Josie interrupted. She glanced across the street. "Look who came to town." Viktor stood there on the sidewalk, shoulders slouched, towering over a small man dressed in painter's clothes. White shirt, white pants. The brim of his white cap shadowed most his face. "I think that's one of the men who were painting when we came.

Nice guy. We met the day that I moved in." Josie stuck two fingers in her mouth, and whistled long and loud. "Hey," she called. "It's me. Josie. We met at Sparrow Road." At the table next to ours, a group of teen girls snickered.

The painter rested one hand on his cap brim; he stared hard for a second like he wasn't really sure who Josie was. Then Viktor touched his shoulder, turned him so their backs were facing us.

"Hey, it's me!" Josie called again, but they didn't listen. Their heads were close in secret conversation. Finally, the painter glanced over his shoulder; then without a word or wave to Josie he turned and walked away. A few steps down the street he stopped, looked at us again, and gave a little wave. A hint of wave, but I saw it just the same.

"Weird," Josie said. "He was friendly when we met."

Viktor crossed the street and headed straight for us. "Is your mother with you, Raine?" He didn't say a word to Josie.

"No." I looked over at the girls. I didn't want anyone to see me with the Iceberg. His rumpled clothes. His uncombed hair. The whiskers on his face. "We rode bikes to Comfort."

"But she knows that you're here?" It was bad enough to have people stare too long at Josie, but now these girls were watching me. Watching ragged Viktor Berglund talk to me like I was ten. Not twelve. Not going on thirteen. Leif was probably watching from the window.

"She does indeed," Josie interrupted. "Raine's finally been set free."

"We rode in for root beer floats," I said. "It's fine."

"Well then," he said. "If the root beer floats are finished, I shall put your bike into my truck and take you home."

"Viktor, we can bike." Josie smashed her empty cup and tossed it toward the can. I could tell she was annoyed that Viktor had ignored her, and I knew it hurt her feelings when the painter turned away. Josie wasn't too familiar with unfriendly. "Raine and I have business here in town."

"Josie, you may bike," Viktor directed. "Or you may ride with me. But Raine will go home now." First Mama and now Viktor? What right did Viktor Berglund have to take me home from town?

"No," I said. Both Leif and Dave were watching from the window. "I want to stay." We still had our memories to make, and Marge's lemon bars, and trinkets from the five-and-dime to buy.

"No," Viktor ordered. "It's best I drive you home."

When we pulled into the driveway, Mama and Diego were sitting on the steps. A look of sudden dread shadowed Mama's face. "What's wrong?" she called. She was at my door before I even had it opened. "Did something happen, Raine?"

"I'm returning Raine from Comfort," Viktor said, as if I were a package he picked up off the street.

Mama pressed her palm against her chest. "Is everything okay? Where's Josie?"

"Josie stayed," I snapped. I wanted Mama to know that I was mad. "Without me." By now, Josie was probably at the Blue Moon eating lemon bars with Marge, telling her about the Arts Extravaganza.

"Well, I'm glad to see you home," Mama said. She put her arms out for a hug, but I just stepped away. I was too old to be taken home from Comfort like a kid.

"He *made* me leave," I said to Mama. "And there wasn't any reason."

"Molly," Viktor said. "If I might be permitted to explain."

"I should have stayed with Josie." I crossed my arms over my stomach. "I'm not a little kid. I'm twelve. I'm going to be thirteen."

"I know," Mama said. "But—"

"That's right!" Diego interrupted. He walked up and rested both his hands on Mama's shoulders. "This girl is growing up. And hey, she looks okay to me. Safe and sound. No alien abduction after all." Diego laughed his big deep laugh, but none of us laughed with him.

Viktor nodded toward his office. "Molly, if I might have a minute?"

Mama looked at Viktor and I saw that strange worry flash back through her eyes. "Sweetheart." Mama touched my elbow, but I yanked my arm away. "I'm sorry you're upset. The next time you go to town, I'll take you in with me."

"What?" I said. "The Rhubarb Social is tomorrow. I'm biking in with Josie and Diego. It's already been planned."

"Oh, *that*." Mama sighed. "I don't know about that social."

"Why? Mama, I can't miss it. We're making rhubarb taffy. Josie and I have a recipe invented. There isn't any danger in that town. It's safe. You know that, Mama."

"The silence rule," Viktor scolded like he suddenly remembered; but it was only me he wanted to be quiet. "Perhaps we can observe it now that Raine is clearly safe."

He pointed toward his office. "Molly, if I might have a minute?"

"I guess that's my cue to leave," Diego joked, but I could tell he didn't want Mama going off with Viktor. He gave my ponytail a little tug. "On a brighter note," he said. "We have a date tonight. The three of us."

"A date?" I said. Mama didn't have dates. Not with anyone. Not ever. How did Diego get Mama to say yes?

Viktor flinched like he wished he hadn't heard Diego just say date.

"Not a date," Mama blurted. Her cheeks burned red. "It's not a date at all."

"Okay, not a date." Diego winked at me. "Maybe a date was too much wishful thinking. We have an *outing*. An outing on the lake. Butter-brickle ice cream in a rowboat with the stars."

"The silence, please." Viktor stepped away. "Molly, in my office."

"Yes," Mama said. "I know."

Mama was a long time in Viktor's office—so long I walked back to our cottage, climbed the stairs up to my bed, slid my sketchbook from my mattress, and told Lyman the terrible story of my day. Lyman was half diary, half person—someone who would listen, and someone who would talk.

What's wrong? I wrote. *Why does Mama make me stay so close? Why won't she let me go like other kids? Why was she worried about Comfort?*

I waited, but Lyman wouldn't answer.

Lyman? I closed my eyes. My lids were hot, my skin itched from the heat. Everything about the day seemed fever strange—the long bike ride through the valley, Josie's crazy plan for the Arts Extravaganza, the painter on the street, the way he turned back and barely waved. Mama's sudden date. Viktor forcing me to leave while everybody watched.

Why did Viktor make me leave? Why didn't he let me stay in town with Josie? What are he and Mama talking about now? Why did Mama move us here this summer? What secret are they hiding in that town?

Well, there has to be a story, Lyman finally said.

I know, I said. *But what?*

What was or what could be? Lyman said. *Dream. Maybe your answer will be there.*

Maybe, I wrote. Then I dropped my sketchbook on the floor and fell asleep.

I woke to muffled voices floating through my window. Mama and Diego, their talk more murmurings than words.

"I can't blame Viktor for today," Mama said. "He was only trying to help. He knows I want to handle this my way. In my own time."

"Still," Diego said. "Did he need to bring her home?"

"It was probably for the best," Mama said. "At least until Raine knows; and I want to do it right. When I'm certain Raine is ready."

"But isn't that the reason why you came here in the first place?"

"It hasn't even been two weeks," Mama said. "I wanted Raine to settle in at Sparrow Road before I told her."

Told me what? Mama's voice sounded serious, like something horrible was ahead. Like Grandpa Mac was sick. Or maybe something worse.

"I think she's settled in," Diego said. "Are you sure it's Raine who isn't ready?"

At first Mama didn't answer. "You're right," she finally said. "It's me."

"I know it's tough, but you can do it, Molly." Diego sounded like he had the day he'd helped me climb the ladder. "You can. And a good time would be now."

When I heard our screen door slam, I lay there still as stone. Downstairs Mama opened the old refrigerator and poured herself a drink. Lemonade. We always had a pitcher in our refrigerator here. Fresh lemonade with blueberries on top.

"Hey," I called. The heat from the low ceiling pressed against my skin. I couldn't stay up here much longer.

"Raine?" Mama sounded shocked. Before I could go down, she hurried up the steps. "Why are you here in bed in the middle of the day?"

"I fell asleep. Why were you so long in Viktor's office?" I rolled my eyes; I wanted her to know my anger hadn't passed.

Mama sat down on my bed. "A nap? Sweetheart, are you okay? Are you sick from that long bike ride?" She pressed her icy hand against my forehead. "Looks like a storm is on the way. It's a good thing Viktor brought you home."

"It's not," I said. "And that's not why he made me leave."

"Lemonade?" She offered me her glass. I shook my head; my stomach did feel sick. "It's like an oven in here, Raine."

"Why'd you bring me here?" I said to Mama.

"Here?" Mama glanced away.

"To Sparrow Road. I just heard Diego say it. He said it's why we came to Sparrow Road. That thing you should have told me. And why did Viktor take me back from town?"

"Oh, Raine." Mama scooted closer. "I know some things seem strange here."

"More than some," I said. "But you won't ever tell me."

"Telling isn't always easy, Raine." Mama combed her fingers through my hair. "Sometimes the truth isn't always what you want. Even when you ask for it."

"I want the truth today," I said.

Another flash of worry passed over her tight face. "I know you do." She gave my hand a squeeze. "But I'm not sure where to start."

"Just start at the beginning. Why we're here? What's going on with Viktor? Why'd he drive me home from Comfort?"

"All right." Mama heaved a heavy sigh. "I'll start with why we're here."

Mama said it was a story we had to settle in for, a story she couldn't tell me in the weight of all this heat, so first she made us go downstairs. Outside, the meadow sky was a sickly shade of green. "The calm before the storm," Mama said as she closed the cottage door and latched the lock. Then she sat down on the couch and took a long, slow breath. "You know how mad Grandpa Mac was about this job? How upset he was with me the day he drove us to the train?"

"Yes," I said. Even now, his letters only came for me. "He didn't want us to leave."

"He didn't," Mama agreed. "He certainly did not." Storm darkness loomed over the room. Drops of rain plinked against the roof. "But mostly Grandpa Mac was mad because there was someone here he didn't want you to meet."

"Here?" I said, confused. The only people here to worry Grandpa Mac would be Eleanor or Viktor, but Grandpa Mac didn't know either one.

"Sweetheart." Mama tucked my hands inside of hers. "You have a——" She stopped like the word was stuck down in her throat. "I mean—you have a father, Raine." She pressed hard on my hands like she was afraid I'd pull away, run out in the storm.

People think we didn't have parents. We had parents. Lyman's voice echoed in my brain. I had a father. Everybody did. "I know," I said, like it wasn't even news. I didn't want Mama to know how much it made my throat ache to hear her finally say it, after years and years of saying that I didn't.

"You do?" Mama reared her head back in surprise.

"I guess," I said. "I know I have one someplace. Everybody does."

"Oh," Mama stammered. "Yes, of course. Of course you'd know that, Raine."

A gust of wind blew back the kitchen curtains and thunder shook the walls. The sky moved from day to night.

"So?" I said. "Is that the person Grandpa Mac didn't

want me to meet? Him?" I couldn't stop my heart from pounding, so fast and hard I heard it in my ears.

"Yes." Mama's eyes held mine. "Yes," she said again.

That man was here at Sparrow Road? "Is it Diego?" I heard the hope squeak out in my voice; Diego would be the perfect dad. Maybe that's why he told Mama she should tell me. And why he'd asked about my dad the first day that we met. And why he spent all that time with Mama. Maybe Mama brought me here to meet Diego. "Mama, is it him?"

"Diego?" Mama gave a small, sad smile. "No, but Diego would be lovely, Raine."

Suddenly my heart lurched inside my chest. If my dad wasn't Diego, that only left one man. I slapped my hands over my ears; I didn't want to hear it. Not another word. The root beer float rose up in my stomach. "I don't want to know," I said.

"Raine." Mama rubbed a circle on my back. "Sweetheart, you said that you were ready for the truth."

"But I don't want it to be Viktor." His name came out like a choke. My father was the Iceberg. A silent, sunken man as old as Grandpa Mac.

"Viktor?" Mama's eyes grew huge. "Oh, heavens!" She shook her head. "Raine, it isn't Viktor!"

"No?" I let my hands drop from my ears. "You're sure?"

"Absolutely." Mama gave a little laugh. "I'm sure it isn't Viktor."

"Then who?" There wasn't another man at Sparrow Road.

Mama stared out at the storm. "Gray," she finally said. "Gray James."

"Gray James?" The words sounded like the weather. "Gray James? Is that some kind of name?"

"Yes," Mama said. "It's *his* name."

"Gray James?" I said again, confused. "But I don't know him, Mama."

"Not yet." Mama lifted up my chin. "But he wants to know you, Raine."

For the first few minutes, Mama let me sit in silence with that name. Gray James. It was a name I'd never heard. Not anywhere. Not at Sparrow Road. Not even in Milwaukee.

"He's here?" I shook my head. "Where?" I stood up and looked out the open window. The storm had settled some, a bruised sky stretched over the field. Gray James wasn't here at Sparrow Road. Wasn't living in the attic or in some silent wing. If he was here, I would have seen him.

"In Comfort," Mama said.

"In Comfort? Gray James lives in Comfort? Is that why you wouldn't let me go to town? Why Viktor took me home today? So Gray James wouldn't see me? Or so I wouldn't see him?"

Mama gave a guilty nod. "More or less," she said. "Yes. All those things."

"But why didn't you just tell me? Right from the beginning?"

"It's complicated, Raine. Gray and I have things we still need to resolve. Grown-up things. And I needed to be ready."

"Ready for what, Mama?"

"I don't know." Mama looked up at the ceiling. "The changes this will bring. Sharing you with Gray, I guess. I know that it sounds selfish, but sharing you with Grandpa Mac has been enough. And our life has been so happy. At least it has been for me." The way that Mama said it made a lump grow in my throat. "And now all that could change."

"It'll still be happy, Mama." I didn't want Gray James to change my happy life.

"I suppose," Mama said, like she wasn't quite so sure. "We just have to see what happens next. What you want to do now that you know."

"Do?" I said.

"Yes," Mama said. "You're old enough to make up your own mind. I shouldn't be in the middle anymore."

"Me?" I said again. "Gray James is up to me?"

"Yes," Mama said. "You and Gray will have to work it out."

"But how?" I said. Gray James was a stranger.

Suddenly another wave of storm pounded on our cottage, with balls of hail pelting past our windows. Outside looked like a blizzard in July. The whine of the old refrigerator stopped.

"I hope it's not a sign!" Mama said. Up at the main house, all the lights were out. A wall of darkness everywhere and it wasn't even night. Mama lit two candles and set them on the table.

If I ever sewed a memory patch, I knew what mine would be—Viktor's truck and hail and root beer floats and Josie, how hot it was this morning biking through the valley. And behind it all a mystery. Gray James? I'd stitch his name in secret letters, or in little tiny print only I could see.

"But who is he?" I asked. Once, I overheard Grandpa Mac tell Mr. Sheehan that Mama got mixed up with a man who wasn't worth a dime. A no-good we were better off without. And sometimes after that, I worried he might have been in prison, dangerous, or else Mama would have told me who he was. "I mean, more than just his name? What kind of person is he?"

Mama stiffened. "What do you want to know exactly?"

"I don't know. Like is he dangerous? Could he hurt us in some way? Hurt me?" I'd held that fear inside for so long it almost hurt to say it.

"Oh no." Mama brushed my cheek. "Not dangerous. Not in the ways you mean. Most the harm Gray's done, he's done to himself." Mama pressed her lips against my forehead. "In fact, you have his gentle spirit, Raine."

It felt strange to hear Mama say I came from someone else, someone who wasn't an O'Rourke. Maybe I'd inherited his black hair and crooked teeth? His big dark eyes? Maybe he was short like me? So little of my looks came down from Grandpa Mac or Mama. Mama cupped my face with her soft hands. "I've always seen him in you, Raine. Every day since your beginning. All the things I loved about Gray James live inside you."

"You loved him, Mama?" If Mama loved him why weren't they together? Why didn't she ever say his name? Why didn't she want him in our life?

"Of course I did," Mama said. "I loved him for a long, long time."

21

Mama and I stayed camped out in our cottage, the electricity still down, with peanut butter sandwiches and apples for a snack. Mama told me Gray James was a musician from Missouri. A folk singer famous in some circles for the sad songs that he sang. She said they'd met in Amsterdam when she was singing on the street. "My hippie days." She shook her head. "Back when I was living on that boat."

"Before we moved back to Milwaukee to live with Grandpa Mac?"

"Yes," Mama said.

"Well, if you loved him, why didn't you get married?"

"Oh, Raine." Mama blushed, embarrassed. It was a blush that made me worry that Mama was in this love alone. "I don't want to talk about those things."

"But did he disappear? I mean, all these years, where was he?"

Mama stared into my eyes, the kind of long look she gave before she told me something serious. "Gray has things he plans to tell you for himself. It's not for me to say." She lifted up our dirty plates and walked over to the sink.

"But why?" I said. "And if he wasn't really dangerous, why didn't I ever know him before now? Not even his name? Or that he was a singer from Missouri? Things you could've told me."

"I could have." Mama stared out at the meadow. "And I know you think I should have. But I wanted you to have a family you could count on. Stable. Steady. And I couldn't count on Gray. Plus Grandpa Mac didn't want him in our life. I thought the family that we built would be enough."

"It was," I said. "But I wish he hadn't been a mystery. I wish I would have known his name at least."

"I'm sorry," Mama said. "But what I did, I did with love."

It wasn't until Diego showed up at our cottage with a plate of oatmeal cookies that Mama remembered the artists needed supper and I remembered that Diego said we had a date out on the lake.

"We already ate," Diego said. "A feast of leftovers and cookies we scrounged out of the freezer. The electricity's still down. And I'm afraid the butter-brickle ice cream melted to a mess. But we can still go on the boat."

Mama wrapped her arm around my back. "We're not up for company tonight. It's been a big day here." The way she said *big day*, I knew she was sending a signal to Diego.

Diego nodded like he knew the truth was finally told. He stepped back from the cottage. "In that case, our rowboat ride can wait." He took a little bow and set the plate of cookies in my hand. "And Raine, Josie said to tell you that the rhubarb taffy's still a go."

"The rhubarb taffy!" In all this talk of Gray James, I'd forgotten the Rhubarb Social was tomorrow. Our rhubarb taffy still needed to be made.

"But first you'll need electricity," Diego said. "Josie plans to brew it bright and early. She'll probably be at your door at sunrise."

"Oh," Mama moaned like she was sick. "That Rhubarb Social is tomorrow." I knew now why Mama didn't want us to go. Gray James lived in town. "We might just stay home."

"No," I said. "I have to go. We've been planning it all week." Josie said there'd be people at the picnic who remembered when the orphans lived at Sparrow Road. Maybe someone who knew Lillian. Someone who could tell us the way things used to be.

"Josie's got everybody going," Diego said to Mama. "Even Lillian and Viktor."

"Eleanor?" I asked.

"No." Diego laughed. "I don't think she recruited Eleanor."

Mama pulled me closer. "Tomorrow's just too early. Raine doesn't even know when or where or *if* she wants to meet him." Mama had said that just because Gray lived as close as Comfort didn't mean I'd have to meet him if it wasn't what I wanted now.

"Of course," Diego said. "Raine will need more time. But that doesn't mean she has to miss the Rhubarb Social."

"But what if Gray is there?" Mama said. "Eating rhubarb pie? And the two of them just meet? I want Raine to have a choice. To meet him when she's ready."

Tomorrow *was* too early; after twelve long years without him, I needed time to get used to Mama's news. Figure out what I wanted next. But I didn't want to miss the Rhubarb Social either. I'd already had one good day with Josie ruined. "Mama," I said. "We've been planning this all week. Can't you call him on the phone? Ask him not to go?"

"I can try," Mama said. "If you're sure that's what you want."

"Wow!" Josie whistled. "This is quite a crowd for Comfort. You ready for a party, Raine?" She pulled our tins of rhubarb taffy from her backpack and set them on the table with every other rhubarb recipe the folks from Comfort cooked.

"Sure," I said. I was, but not as ready as I had been before Gray James became a name, a *what-if* as close as Comfort. Now I mostly had him on my mind.

"Well, we're the only rhubarb taffy!" Josie said. There was rhubarb crisp and rhubarb ice cream, rhubarb bars and cookies, rhubarb cake and bread, rhubarb soup and rhubarb tea brewing in the sun. "We win for originality at least!"

"True." I tried to smile. It might have been original, but our taffy tasted terrible—sweet and sour and stringy. I was glad my name wasn't on the tins.

"Come on." Josie yanked my arm. "Let's go make some friends!"

The two of us worked the Rhubarb Social as a pair while Mama watched us from a table in the shade. She kept her worried eyes on me like Gray James just might be here after all.

"And this would be our writer, Raine," Josie said to everyone we met. She dragged me through the picnic and made me shake so many hands I felt like I was running for election.

Most the men I saw made me think about Gray James. Was he somewhere at this picnic? Would I shake his hand by accident and not know it was him? That singer from Missouri? That gentle spirit Mama couldn't count on?

"We're from Sparrow Road," Josie said to everybody. "The artist retreat. Raine writes. Me, I sew fabric art from scraps. Quilty kinds of things." For some reason, the quilting part put most folks at ease. The ladies talked to Josie about their own quilts they were sewing; a couple of men asked about my stories. Everyone we met took a few odd looks at Josie. "Reuse and recycle," Josie joked whenever someone stared too long at her dress. Still, I could tell they liked the happy gap between her teeth and the kind way she offered everyone our terrible rhubarb taffy.

We sat down at table after table, and at every table Josie invited strangers to our Arts Extravaganza. In just one day, the Arts Extravaganza had turned real. Real, but Viktor still didn't know. Mama either. I was glad they sat far enough away that they couldn't hear Josie's plans.

"So you'll come?" Josie asked at the end of every conversation. "We can count on you?" Most folks didn't seem eager, but everyone was too polite to say so. The Comfort folks were a distant kind of friendly—nice enough, but not in any hurry to have you to their house. Not Josie's brand of friendly.

Whenever Mama caught my eye, she'd pat the empty seat beside her. She already had Diego, Lillian, and Viktor, but I knew it was me she wanted close in case Gray James suddenly appeared. Mama wanted me to sit, but I just couldn't. We still had our research to get done.

"Did you know any of the orphans?" I asked a man who looked as shaky old as Lillian.

"Well, no," he rasped. "I can't say that I did. Although they came to church on holidays, of course. A few hitched rides on the highway when they tried to run away."

"Run away?" I asked.

"I suppose to get back to where they came from. They weren't original to Comfort. Never were. We're not a town of orphans. Children here have parents. We're a family kind of place." He squinted at the sun. Across the lawn a group of kids played a game of rhubarb toss.

"Good invention," Josie said to me. "Rhubarb toss. We'll need good games at our Arts Extravaganza."

"You know." He tapped his cane against my leg. "There may be one orphan. A lady in Spring Valley. Married to a Lutheran preacher. I believe she settled in these parts."

"A lady in Spring Valley?" Josie jumped out of her seat. "Any chance you know her name?"

"Nope," he said. "I can't say that I do."

When I turned back to Mama's table she was gone. Viktor too. There were people crowded everywhere, families gathered on old blankets, but Mama wasn't anywhere in sight.

"I'll be right back," I said to Josie. Mama's sudden absence made me certain something strange was going on.

"Where'd Mama go?" I asked Diego. "And Viktor?" I had a hunch Gray James was at this picnic and Mama was somewhere at his side.

"How's the research going?" Diego joked like he hadn't heard my question. "I think you and Josie better plan to run the world." He reached into his pocket and pulled out a purple bead. "My big find so far at this picnic. Must be left over from a Sunday school project."

"Oh, Sunday school." Lillian pointed toward Good Shepherd. "Our children never go to Sunday school in town. But of course we always pray."

"Diego?" I interrupted.

"More rhubarb tea, sweet Lilly?" Diego picked up her empty cup.

"Is he here?" I asked Diego. Everywhere there were men in Sunday suits. Men in ties. Men in sport shirts and long sleeves. Men in baseball caps and glasses. Somewhere out there Mama was talking to Gray James. I knew it in my heart. "Tell me."

"He was." Diego finally nodded. "But I believe your mama asked him to go home."

That night after the social, I pestered Mama with my questions. Even though she said Gray didn't see me at the picnic, I couldn't escape the feeling that I'd missed him by a minute. The answer to a question I'd wondered my whole life. He'd been there in the crowd, then he was gone. A man I could have met by accident, and all of my decisions would be done.

The little Mama told me—how he grew up in a trailer in Missouri, how he made records for a living, how his melancholy songs went straight to people's hearts—she told me in a hurry, like Gray James was a subject she couldn't dwell on for too long.

Did you think about your father's face? I wrote Lyman the next morning. Lyman knew the feeling of having someone gone. *Wonder what he looked like?* I closed my eyes and imagined Lyman sitting right beside me, the two of us just talking at Viktor's turtle pond. The white sun waving in the water. The timid turtles sunning on the rocks. Turtles were the perfect pets for Viktor.

Sure, Lyman said. *I saw him in my mind. And other times when I looked into the mirror. I liked to think I saw his face in mine. But who knows, he might not have looked like me at all. But you're a girl,* he said. *A girl would take after her mother.*

I know my mother, I said. *And we don't look alike.*

Then I guess you take after him. Lyman ran his fingers through the water. It was too slimy green and murky for me to ever touch. *But you'll see that for yourself when you meet him face-to-face.*

Three days had passed since I learned about Gray James, and still I didn't know when or how or if the two of us would meet.

You think we'll really meet? I asked.

Sure, he said. *If I were you, I'd want to meet him now.*

It was late that afternoon when Viktor found me in the tower. He reached his pale, skinny arm up through the trapdoor and without a word left a wrinkled envelope beside me on the floor. Sealed, so I knew he hadn't read it. In blocky penciled letters on the front someone had written RAINE O'ROURKE. All capitals, just like every word printed in the letter.

DEAR RAINE,
I BET YOU THINK IT'S LATE FOR ME
TO COME KNOCKING AT YOUR DOOR.
I CAN ONLY SAY IT'S SOMETHING
IN MY LIFE I NEED TO SET RIGHT,
AND I'M SORRY FOR MOST THE THINGS
I'VE DONE. THE THINGS THAT HURT
YOU ESPECIALLY. I COULD GO ON
AND ON HERE ABOUT MISTAKES AND
LIFE, ETC., BECAUSE I AM SUPPOSED
TO HAVE A GIFT WITH WORDS, BUT
I DO BETTER WHEN I'M PUTTING
THOUGHTS INTO MUSIC. BETTER STILL
IF IT'S NOT MY OWN HEARTACHE I'M
TRYING TO GET ON PAPER. I AM HERE
IN COMFORT, NOT FAR FROM SPARROW
ROAD. YOUR MAMA SAYS YOU'LL SEE
ME WHEN YOU'RE READY. I AM READY
WHEN YOU ARE.
                    YOUR FRIEND,
                    Gray James

Only his name was signed in messy cursive. *Gray*, he
wrote, not *Dad*, which felt exactly right to me. Gray James—
who would be ready when I was.

. . .

I must have read that letter fifty times at least. I read it in the tower and underneath the willow, alone out in the meadow, on the dock down at the lake. I read it by the moonlight, before I fell asleep. Gray James. It was a voice I'd been missing for so long. Him. My whole life mystery. And here he was knocking at my door. Saying he was sorry. The secret hope I'd carried in my heart.

The day after Gray's letter a record came for me.

I was tucked under the willow writing all of this to Lyman, every mixed-up feeling, when Viktor lifted back the leaves and asked to see me in his office.

Inside the old infirmary, a dusty phonograph was set up on his desk. Viktor held up a faded record album jacket. "Gray asked me to deliver this to you." Then he slid the record out, set it on the phonograph, put the needle down, and left me listening alone.

In my dream you are a lost night, Gray James sang.

I picked up the cardboard cover and stared down at a scruffy sort of cowboy in the back end of a truck. A cigarette in one hand, a bottle of beer held up in the other. His ragged jeans were ripped and stained, his old white T-shirt wrinkled. His cowboy boots were crusted thick with mud. His shy eyes were brown like mine, his straight black hair hung loose around his face. He looked a lot like me. A lot like me.

Lost Time was written on the bottom.

Lies are lies even when I tell them. Gray James's voice was gravelly and lonesome; I could see why he was famous in some circles for his melancholy songs. Every sad word was a man missing something he couldn't name. A lost man walking down a highway. *Whatever home was, it ain't home now.*

For a long time, I sat in Viktor's dusty office staring at Gray's face and listening to him sing. The hurting ran so deep his music almost made me cry. Song after song stirred some kind of horrible sorrow in my stomach. It made me think of Lillian and Lyman. All the orphans. How long they waited for their parents. But most of all, it made me ache for Grandpa Mac.

I lifted the needle from the record, picked up the phone, and called Grandpa Mac collect.

"Raine?" Grandpa sounded frantic. "Is everything okay?"

"I know about Gray James," I blurted out.

"So I heard," Grandpa Mac growled. Mama must have talked to Grandpa Mac. I didn't think the two of them had spoken since the day we left Milwaukee.

"I haven't met him yet," I said. "But I guess he wants to meet." I looked down at the shabby cowboy's picture. His face was young-boy sweet, like he hadn't grown up to Mama's age. "I'm not sure if I should." I bit my lip and waited. I wanted Grandpa Mac to say it was okay, to let me know he'd love me whatever I decided.

"That makes two of us, sweetheart." Grandpa Mac's breath sounded worn out and long. "You're still a little girl."

"I'm not little, Grandpa Mac. I'm going to be thirteen."

"Sweetheart, you could have gone your whole life without this yahoo."

Yahoo. When Grandpa Mac said it, the name seemed to fit Gray James. A drinking and smoking cowboy in the back end of a truck. I stared down at the picture. "Mama said that he was safe."

"Well, your mama thinks she knows," Grandpa Mac said, like he thought Mama was wrong.

"So do you want me to say no?" I knew Grandpa Mac would tell it to me straight.

I waited through his heavy breaths. "I want you to come home," he finally said. "Get it straightened out on this end. Not in Timbuktu with a bunch of kooky artists. Let that yahoo deal with me here. Your mother's done her share of crazy things, but this—"

"Don't be mad at Mama. Please." I didn't want Grandpa Mac to hold Gray James against Mama, just like I didn't want him to hold Gray James against me.

"I'm not mad," Grandpa Mac lied. "This just isn't any way to raise a child. You've got a first-class family—your mom and I, Lord, we love you more than life. That ought to be enough."

"It is." I felt worse than when I'd first picked up the phone. Somehow calling Grandpa Mac had only made my decision that much harder. "So will you be mad at me? If I decide to see him? 'Cause I don't want you to be mad."

"I'm never mad at you, Raine."

"I know," I said. But that wasn't quite the same as saying that he wouldn't be. I pressed Gray's album cover to my chest. "He sings."

"Lots of people sing. That doesn't make them saints." Grandpa Mac put his hand over the phone. Through the muffle, I could hear he had a customer waiting to check out. "Sweetheart, have your mother call me, please. Will you do that for me?"

My heart sank. Calling Grandpa Mac had only made the trouble between him and Mama worse. And Gray James was in the middle, just like me.

"Sweetheart?"

My throat hurt too much to speak. One word to Grandpa Mac and a flood of tears would be streaming down my face.

Whatever home was, it ain't home now. Gray's sad song was already in my soul.

"Raine?" Grandpa Mac's voice softened just a little. "Come home," he said. "We'll get it all worked out."

"That's one wistful picture," Josie whispered. "So much longing there. So much wishing on that page."

The two of us stared at Lyman's drawing. Other artwork was taped up in the attic, but Lyman's drawing was the one that always made us dream. Waves of stark white hills covered in a perfect sheet of snow. Not a single footprint. It had the forlorn feeling of a wish. The way I felt when I wondered about Gray.

All of it was wistful: Lyman's snowy hills, Gray's music, the orphans' empty beds, the single slice of moon outside the attic. My heart when I looked at Gray James's album. My call to Grandpa Mac. Longing. I knew what Josie meant. "It's like the sound in Gray James's songs," I said.

"Really?" Josie kept her eyes on Lyman's picture. "His songs are wistful, huh?"

"Yep," I said. "His record's called *Lost Time*."

"Well, that's one wistful title," Josie said. "I bet Gray James had some trouble in his heart. Lots of folks put sorrow in their art. And art's the perfect place to put it." Josie dropped backward on the bed. "Maybe he was dreaming of the time he lost with you."

"No," I said. "He could have come to see me. I was always in Milwaukee."

"Well, there must have been some reason," Josie said. "If I had you as my daughter, I wouldn't want to miss a minute." She rolled over on her stomach and propped her chin against her fist. "But at least you'll get to ask him."

"Maybe I shouldn't meet him. Grandpa Mac and Mama are my family. That ought to be enough."

"Sure," Josie said. "But you got room for more. Everybody does. Like us. Already we're a kind of summer family. The more family you let in, the happier you'll be."

"But Grandpa Mac—" I thought about my phone call. The sick swirl in my stomach the second we hung up. "He definitely doesn't want me to meet Gray."

"No?" Josie frowned. "Well, some folks hold the things they love too close. Maybe that's the case with Grandpa Mac. But from all the stories that you tell me, I'm pretty certain it's your happiness he wants." Josie pulled a rock out of her pocket and pressed it in my palm. "My heart stone," she said. "Just hold it tight and listen. Then tell me what your heart is saying to you now."

I squeezed the cold stone in my hand; it felt smooth and round and sturdy. Then I closed my eyes and let the attic silence help me hear my heart.

"I know I want to meet him," I said finally. "Without anybody mad or sad. Grandpa Mac or Mama. Or trouble up ahead. Or my good life to be gone. I just want to know him. See him for myself. And have it turn out happy." I stopped. I wasn't going to cry right there in front of Josie.

"So," Josie said. "Let's invite him to my barbecue this Sunday."

"Your barbecue this Sunday?" I opened up my eyes. Josie still hadn't told Viktor about the Arts Extravaganza, and now she was planning a cookout? Josie's wild mind was a mystery to me.

"It's just a small fiesta I'm hosting for our house," Josie said. "We should probably get to work!" She sprang up from the bed like the cookout was today. "What's summer without ribs and roasted corn and watermelon? And I'll do all the fixing so your mom won't have to fuss."

"Mama and Gray in the same place?" It hadn't even been a week since Mama told me; I didn't get the feeling she was ready for Gray yet. Or at least for Gray with me.

"Sure," Josie said. "And everybody else. Lillian, Diego. All of us who love you, Raine. So you won't have to meet him by yourself."

"You really think he'd come here for a cookout?"

"I do. I think that he'd be honored."

Together we made his invitation. Josie glued glitter on the paper, I asked Gray James to come to Sparrow Road.

As soon as it was finished I gathered up my courage and knocked on Viktor's door.

"A barbecue this Sunday?" Viktor rubbed his hand across his tired eyes.

"Josie is hosting it for everybody." I hoped Viktor would stay in his infirmary; I hoped Eleanor would hide up in her room. "All of us. And Gray can come here, too."

"I'm afraid I hadn't heard." Viktor cleared his throat. "But I expect as much from Josie."

I held out the invitation. "I thought you could deliver it for me. Since you brought the things from Gray."

"But Molly?" Viktor said. "Does she know this invitation's been extended?"

"Sort of." I was on my way to tell her, but first I had to hand it off to Viktor. "Mama said the decision was all mine."

When Sunday came, I couldn't keep my hands from shaking. They trembled from the time I opened up my eyes. A flock of birds beat inside my chest.

What kind of person would he be? What would we say? How would Mama act? Did she still love Gray James? And what about Diego? Ever since the Rhubarb Social, Diego had been at our cottage every night to sit with Mama on the swing. I wondered how he'd feel about a man Mama used to love.

At five o'clock, I put on my favorite jeans and the flowered peasant shirt I bought for sixth-grade pictures. Josie

109

told me I'd feel best dressed as myself. No fancy foo-foo. I left my dark hair long and straight. Looking in the mirror, I was suddenly afraid Gray James might have dreamed about a different daughter. A pretty red-haired miniature of Mama. What if I wasn't the daughter Gray James had in mind?

"You look nice." Mama stood behind me in the mirror. "Very grown up."

"I'm scared."

"Me too." Mama wrapped her arms around me from behind like she was cold. "A little bit, at least. I just hope this answers all your questions in the end."

26

Outside the main house, silver Christmas tinsel sparkled in the branches and the weathered picnic table was covered in a velvet patchwork cloth that looked like Josie's dress. We all had our own embroidered napkins; even G.J. had one now. A glittered WELCOME waited by his plate. All around the yard, tiny candles burned in clear glass jars. "My latest five-and-dime find!" Josie said. "Two hundred candles for three dollars. And all these old jars were just buried in the barn!"

I was relieved Gray James wasn't there yet. Eleanor either. Mama said that if we were lucky Eleanor wouldn't come to the barbecue at all.

Diego poured us each a cup of fruity punch. "Josie's secret recipe," he said with a wink. Strawberry bits floated on the top. "Be careful. She'll probably put us all under a spell."

Mama forced a smile. "Josie sure knows how to throw a party."

"I sure do." Josie grinned. She looked at Viktor. He was underneath the gnarled oak, sitting on the bench with Lillian. "Parties are my specialty," she added, but Viktor only nodded. Strong as she was, I still didn't think she'd get him to agree to the Arts Extravaganza.

"You look so lovely," Lillian said to me. She patted at the empty chair beside her. "Please join me, dear. It's nice here in the shade." She lifted the dainty punch cup to her lips. "In all these years, we've never had a party. Not like this."

"I believe there was a party every Christmas," Viktor said. "With gingerbread you used to bake."

"Did I?" Lillian blinked. "And was the party happy?"

"I don't know." Viktor combed his bony fingers through his hair. "I was a child then. What do children know?"

Viktor was a child at Sparrow Road? Did he visit the orphans with the Berglunds? Or was he an orphan once? Is that why he and Lillian were friends? Was he one of the children?

If I hadn't been so nervous about Gray, I would have jumped out of my seat and rushed the update straight to Josie.

"Children know so many things," Lillian said. She rested her wrinkled hand over my wrist. "This one is a wizard. She reads poetry to me."

It was the grind of tire against gravel that made everybody freeze. My heart stilled in my chest. I couldn't breathe. I *really* couldn't breathe. My voice was gone. The top of my head tingled. When I heard his car door slam, I wanted to bolt into the house, climb up to the tower, and slide the lock across the latch.

"He's here," Mama said. She looked at me as if it were the last time that she'd see me. I wanted her to hug me, to hold me until my heart slowed, but she stood frozen like a statue near the punch.

"Gray arrives," Viktor announced. He glanced at me. Josie and Diego looked at me. Lillian was staring at the lilies.

I shrugged. "Okay," I squeaked. I didn't feel it, or mean it, but I said it because I didn't know what else to say. More words wouldn't have made it out my mouth.

"I enjoy a summer garden," Lillian said.

And then Gray James walked into our yard.

He was small. Not small like me, but closer to Mama's height than Viktor's or Diego's. Small shouldered and small boned. I saw right away I had his scrawny body. Shaggy bangs fell over his eyes. He wore cowboy boots and faded jeans, just like on the album, and his cowboy boots were still caked with crusty mud. Mama said he was her age, but he looked more like a boy. A battered old guitar case dangled from one hand.

"Hey there," he said to nobody, and his voice had that same slow twang of his songs.

"Gray," Viktor said. He ambled over and set his hand down on Gray's small shoulder, almost the way a father would. Mama just stood silent. "You're right on time. Let me introduce our summer artists: Diego, Lillian, and Josie." Gray nodded toward each person. "Eleanor hasn't joined us yet."

"I met you my first day!" Josie stepped forward and swallowed up Gray's hand. "When you were here working on the house. Painting those old windows." Painting? Was Gray the painter we saw with Viktor on the street? The small man who barely waved? Wasn't he a singer anymore? "Well, how cool that you're Raine's—" Josie stumbled on her sentence, then she stopped. "Raine's Gray."

"Glad to be." Gray gave a little grin. Then he turned to Mama and tried to hand her the shabby old guitar case. "It's an old Martin I picked up at a pawn shop. For you." He looked shy and scared and small in front of Mama, and Mama didn't look happy to see him.

"Great gift," Diego said. He shook Gray's hand. "I can't wait to hear her play."

"Thanks," Mama said to Gray, but she wouldn't take it. "But I don't play guitar anymore."

"Yeah," Gray said. "You told me. But that's a terrible shame. So I did a little shopping." He held it out to Mama until she gave in and took it from his hand.

"Raine?" Mama called. She motioned for me to stand up from my lawn chair, to come over and say hello to Gray

James, but my legs were too weak to walk across the yard. Instead, I pulled my knees up to my chest, wrapped my hands around my flip-flops, and waited while Gray James followed Mama to my chair. I wanted a giant box to drop over my body. A fishbone was trapped inside my throat.

Gray James sank his hands in his back pockets. "Raine?" he said. His black deer eyes had a little bit of Lillian's confusion, like he wasn't completely certain who I was.

"She's waiting for her father," Lillian said.

My cheeks washed red; I didn't want Gray James to think I was waiting here for him.

Gray grinned. "That so?" he said to Lillian. "Well, that's good news for me."

"Okay," Mama gulped before she left us. "I'm going to get more punch."

27

Gray sat down next to Lillian. "Hey," he said to her, but he kept his smile on me. "Raine?" He shook his head a little. When he said my name it sounded like a question. "I hardly can believe it."

"This one is a gift," Lillian said. She touched my sleeve. "She reads poetry to me. I didn't write poetry until after I was sixty." Lillian ran her wrinkled hand over her book.

"Well, good for you." Gray grinned. His shy, crooked smile never left his face. "Oh," he said. He reached into the pocket of his shirt. "I got something for you, too." He handed me a tiny box tied closed with curly ribbon. "You don't have to open it right now."

"Thanks," I said. I tried to sound more sincere than Mama.

Mama propped the guitar against the table, then disappeared into the house. A second later Diego went in too. Josie lined the ears of corn up on the grill. "I hope everybody's hungry," Josie said.

Gray bent forward and rested his elbows on his knees. His skin was tan like mine, olive, but with tiny specks of paint. "You surely are a sight." He cupped his hands together and put his cheek down on his fist. "You as scared as me?"

I nodded. One nod and my eyes already watered.

"We don't have to be anything," Gray said. "Not tonight. Or tomorrow. Or the next day. Or ever, if that's what you decide."

"I'm not sure how long she'll stay," Lillian interrupted. "The little one has hope."

"Hope's good," Gray said. Whenever Lillian added her two cents Gray's eyes lit up, his crooked smile lifted to one side. "Your mama told me some things. You like to read?"

I sounded simple and stupid in Gray's slow country voice. "Sometimes," I said. After all these days of waiting, I didn't have a word to say to Gray. This wasn't how I pictured it at all.

"Raine and I are going to throw a party," Josie blurted suddenly. She was at the grill, a wavy veil of smoke covering her face. "The Arts Extravaganza. So folks can come from Comfort."

"What?" Viktor glared at Josie. "What exactly do you mean?" I could see he was confused. Me too. Why would Josie bring up the Arts Extravaganza now?

"A party!" Josie said. "But bigger than this barbecue. So the folks in Comfort can get to know the good at

Sparrow Road. Can see the art we've created here this summer. We'll make the food ourselves. Plan all the activities. Raine's in charge of games. It won't cost you any money."

"Wow," Gray said. "That's really quite a thing." He leaned back on the bench.

"And you'll come, Gray," Josie ordered. "You'll sing. You and Molly both."

I was glad Mama had gone into the house. She didn't know about the party, didn't know Josie just had invited Gray or that I'd already planned to ask Grandpa Mac to come.

"I don't know about the singing." Gray rubbed his hand across his face. "I'm on a little break."

"And Lillian will read her poetry," Josie said, like Gray would sing regardless. "Eleanor can read from her *masterpiece* if she feels so inclined. Raine is still deciding what she'll make."

"No," Viktor said. "No party."

"Diego and I will open up our sheds. Have our summer work out on display. And everyone who comes will make some art. We'll set up creation stations. Embroidery. Collage. Memory patches. Poetry."

"I will read my poetry," Lillian said.

"Josie," Viktor said. "You can't just plan a party."

"But it won't be any trouble to you." Josie planted her black boots firmly on the ground. She raised her tongs toward Viktor like she was ready for a battle. "And we'll have it on a Sunday. August eighteenth. So it won't interrupt the silence."

"You already chose a date?" Viktor dropped his head.

"Raine and I have been busy making plans."

"Plans?" Viktor sighed.

"And Raine's grandpa will be coming. He's driving from Milwaukee."

"Your grandpa will be coming?" Gray's crooked smile drooped a little bit.

"I hope," I said. I hardly knew my own voice; it felt like I was talking through a tunnel. "I haven't really asked him yet."

"And I will read my poetry," Lillian said again. She pressed her dress down on her legs.

"You see!" Josie said. "The party will be great!" She flipped the ribs and waved the smoke back from her face.

"No party," Viktor said.

"It'll be amazing," Josie said. "An Arts Extravaganza like no other!"

"No," Viktor repeated.

Gray smiled. I could tell he thought Josie was the sun. Strong and bright and big. Maybe strong enough to melt an iceberg. "Hey, Raine," he drawled. "How 'bout we have a walk?"

That walk with Gray was the longest of my life. Gray said his favorite spot at Sparrow Road was the hill that overlooked the lake, because after a long hot day of painting he'd go down and take a dip. "Haven't done it since," he said. "And today is one hot day."

"You don't sing?" I asked. "What about your records?"

"I'm on a break," he said. "Painting houses in between. The steady work helps me dream up songs."

Gray James wasn't a fast talker or a mover. But as we walked across the meadow, my heart started to still, my hands calmed, my old voice was coming back. We didn't talk about us being father-daughter, or Amsterdam or why he never saw me in Milwaukee. His side of the story. Or why Mama never told me who he was. All the mysteries I thought this night would solve. Instead, Gray told about a scrawny near-dead kitten he'd rescued off the road. Mr. Bones. Gray said he'd found him starving and now Mr. Bones liked to sleep draped around Gray's neck like a scarf. And when Gray let him have a taste, he was crazy about cantaloupe. I told him about Beauty, the way she only purred for me and how I bought her a can of tuna every Christmas. I said I hoped I'd have a dog someday, and Gray said that as a boy his best friend had been Buddy, a spaniel mutt his dad won in a poker game. "Shaggy black, with a white stripe down his muzzle." Gray ran his finger down his nose. "Just thinking of that stripe still makes me miss him. I sure wish I had that dog today."

When we finally stopped to look down at the lake, Gray said he wasn't sure about the present. "It may not be a thing a girl would like. I don't know too many girls your age." He tugged a little on his shirt. I'd already forgotten that he gave a gift to me; I'd left the box sitting on my chair. "I spent a lot of hours hunting down the perfect thing. I was so nervous for tonight." Gray let his bangs fall over his face. "But I never did believe something bought could take the place of feelings."

"No," I said. "Me either." I wasn't sure exactly what he meant, but it sounded right to me. Something bought couldn't take the place of feelings. Maybe it was the same thing Grandpa Mac meant when he said money can't buy love. If I'd had the words, I would have told Gray it didn't matter what he bought me. What mattered most, standing there, staring at the lake, was that I had a name and face for my beginning. He was small and slow and sad and kind of country, but I was glad Gray James belonged to me.

It wasn't until our cookout finally ended and Gray James was gone to Comfort, and I was on the swing outside our cottage sitting with the stars, that Josie came to tell me she'd been saving news all week. News she didn't want to tell me while my mind was on Gray James.

"I finally found her, Raine!" Josie clapped her happy hands together. "Nettie Johnson. That preacher's wife over in Spring Valley. The one the man at the Rhubarb Social mentioned. The one who used to be an orphan. Oh, Raine! I finally tracked her down!"

"Whoa!" I said. "That's great." I was glad to think of something besides Gray. All these days of waiting long and wondering had finally worn me out. And I had such a jumbled mix of feelings, I didn't know which feeling to feel first.

"Well, the best part is"—Josie stamped her feet—"Nettie Johnson's coming to Comfort for a chat with you and me! On Friday! A chat and a piece of Blue Moon pie."

"A chat with us?" I couldn't believe Josie had finally found an orphan, someone who really lived at Sparrow Road. I'd been shy with Gray but I'd ask Nettie Johnson every question. What was it like to live at Sparrow Road? Did she know Lillian? Was Lillian an orphan or a teacher? Did she bake gingerbread at Christmas? Did the children really sleep down at the lake? Did all of them find families? Had Viktor Berglund been an orphan too?

When Friday came, Mama walked me to my bike and made me pinkie swear if I saw Gray in Comfort I wouldn't go off with him alone.

"Molly, Molly," Diego laughed. "Raine's safe with me and Josie."

"Safe and sound!" Josie hitched her patchwork dress up to her knees. She always rode like that—dress up, bare legs, big black buckle boots.

"I thought Gray was up to me," I said.

"More or less," Mama sighed. "But you're *my* daughter, Raine. I want to know you're with Josie and Diego."

"Don't worry," I told Mama. For one day, I didn't want the cloud of Mama's fears hanging over me. I wanted peach pie and whatever orphan stories Nettie Johnson had to tell. "I won't go off with Gray."

When we'd finally biked away from Sparrow Road, Diego slowed to pedal right beside me; Josie had already bolted far ahead. "It's a mother bear thing, Raine," Diego panted. Behind him, his Hawaiian shirt flapped back like a bright kite in the breeze. His jet black hair shined blue in the sun. "Your mama's got her claws out for her cub. Mother instinct."

"But Mama said he wasn't dangerous."

"He's not," Diego wheezed. "But people make mistakes. I've made my share along the way." I couldn't picture Diego making a mistake. "Gray let your mama down and that's a hurt that hasn't healed. She just wants to keep your heart safe."

"But Mama needs to let me go," I said. "Things will be okay."

"Probably so," Diego said. "But protection? That's pure mother instinct. Parent instinct. I had it for my boys. And Gray, he's got father instincts of his own." A storm of sweat rained down Diego's face. "He wants the chance to be your dad."

Your dad. No one had ever called Gray James my dad. It sounded foreign and too big to ever fit me. I was glad no one else was there to hear Diego say it. I needed time to wear those words alone.

Nettie Johnson and her husband were at the Blue Moon when we got there and her preacher husband, Reverend Johnson, looked liked anybody else. No black suit or special collar like Father Finnegan would wear. And Nettie didn't look like an orphan. She was gray-haired, short and chubby, with bright pink fingernails, pink lipstick, and a pink sweat suit to match.

"That's quite a head of hair," Reverend Johnson said to Josie. "Reminds me of a rainbow." He slid out of the booth. "I'm off to do my errands, then. I'm not much for sitting with the ladies." Diego wasn't either. He'd given up peach pie to hunt down junk in town. "Be back in a spell," Reverend Johnson said to Nettie.

Our spell with Nettie lasted a long time; it lasted until Marge finally hung the CLOSED sign in the window. She'd already washed our cups and plates, refilled the sugar packet stacks. Nettie told us she was taken to Sparrow Road at two or three, after her mama died from flu. Her father was a soldier in the army, but he never came for her. "I stayed at Sparrow Road until I was fifteen. I wasn't quite adopted," Nettie said. "But there was a farm family in Spring Valley, they took me in to help with their nine kids."

"What about Lillian Hobbs?" I said.

"Lillian Hobbs?" Nettie looked confused.

"She might have been an orphan or a teacher," I said.

Nettie poured another pack of sugar in her coffee. "Hobbs? You mean Miss Hobbs the teacher? Is that the person that you mean?" Nettie Johnson looked surprised. "Very small? Little more than bones? Don't tell me she's alive?"

"She is," Josie said. "Alive and well. At Sparrow Road this summer. So you have to come to see her. In fact we're hosting the Arts Extravaganza on August eighteenth. You and the reverend, we want you both to come. Other orphans too if we can find them. Are you in touch with any?" I couldn't believe Viktor had said yes, but Josie swore to me he did.

"No." Nettie frowned. "Not really. I've left that past behind."

"Did you know Lyman Chase?" Josie asked. "He has a drawing in the attic. Sparrow Road in winter." My heart sank. I hoped Nettie would say no. I wanted Lyman to live in my imagination, just the way I pictured. What if Nettie said that he was mean? Or ugly? Or a boy she always hated? Lyman was safer in my heart.

Nettie shook her head. "Oh no, there were hundreds of us, honey. The orphanage was open for many, many years."

I was relieved she didn't know Lyman. "But what about Viktor Berglund?" I asked.

"Do you mean the Berglunds who gave Sparrow Road to charity? The ones who made it possible for us to have a home?"

"Yes," I said. "Did you ever know a boy named Viktor? He might have been an orphan."

"Viktor?" Josie stared at me wide-eyed. "You really think that, Raine?"

"Could be," I said. "I'm just going on a hunch."

"Berglund? No Berglund was an orphan!" Nettie pressed her hand against her neck. "They were extremely wealthy people who lived off in New York."

"Well, did they ever come at Christmas?" I asked. "The Berglunds? For gingerbread?"

Nettie stared out the café window. Main Street was empty now. "Rich people dropped off presents. Lemon drops. A pomegranate." The pomegranate seemed to make her gloomy. "Sometimes people came to sing. I should go," she said. "The reverend must be waiting."

"You'll come to the party," Josie said. I could tell she didn't want our conversation to end sadly. "August eighteenth. Great food, great art." Josie picked the charge slip off our table. "We want all the orphans to come home."

30

You are a question I will carry
Through Februaries far into my future
Young I can't imagine
how long those winters last

Lillian's eyes were closed, her small hands folded in her lap. We were on the front porch reading *Souvenirs*, a book of Lillian's poetry Viktor dropped off at our cottage. Of all the poems I'd read to Lillian, I liked hers best of all.

"You are a question I will carry," I read again. I didn't always understand them, but I could tell her poems were wistful, like Lyman's drawing or Gray's forlorn songs. Lots of getting left or leaving. A kind of constant homesick in the heart.

"Did your father come yet, dear?" Lillian opened one pink eye. Today Gray was coming for a visit straight from church. He'd asked me in a letter and I sent him back my yes.

"What did this mean?" I asked. *"You are a question I will carry?* Who was the question?"

Lillian closed her eye again like she was drifting back toward sleep.

"In your poem?" I asked. "The question you'll carry into Februaries? The long winter question?"

"Hmm," Lillian murmured, half asleep. "Viktor."

I looked down at the page. *For V.* was written underneath the title. "Viktor? Viktor was a question that you carried?" I gave her arm a little shake. Lillian struggled to bat her eyes awake.

"Did your father come yet, dear?"

"Viktor was a question that you carried?" I asked again.

Lillian straightened up a bit and patted at her hair. "I don't know if I should sit here in this heat."

Parts of Lillian's story were still a mystery to me. Once she was an orphan eating her mother's sausage, and later, as Nettie Johnson said, a teacher. Was she a teacher when she took the children to sleep down at the lake? And what did Viktor have to do with it, besides the fact that the Berglunds gave Sparrow Road to charity?

When Gray's old van pulled into the driveway, I rubbed my thumb along the silver hope charm Gray gave me for a gift. It was a tiny flame with *hope* written in the center and *Raine* engraved across the back. Ever since the barbecue, it hung around my neck on a fragile silver chain. And hope was what I had.

When Gray climbed down from his van, my heart beat harder than it had the night we met. *My dad.* I kept those secret words inside myself. I knew it was too soon to even say them.

"It's him," I said to Lillian. I was glad I had her company. Today, Gray was dressed for Sunday service at Good Shepherd. He wore a crisp white dress shirt and jeans. A thin black tie.

Gray rested his boot against the bottom step. He pushed his bangs back from his face, rubbed his hand under his nose. A week had passed since we first met, and I could tell he was just as nervous to see me again too. Timid grown-ups were always a surprise. I imagined most folks grew up to be as confident as Grandpa Mac and Mama. "Your mama packed a picnic?"

"Uh-huh." It wasn't any easier to talk, or stand, or think the second time I saw him.

"That's sweet." He dropped his hands into his pockets. "Good book?"

"It's Lillian's," I said. "Her poetry. She wrote it."

"That so?" He smiled at Lillian. "I'd like to give that book a read." Maybe Gray could tell me what it meant to carry a question so far into the future. He seemed to understand lost things.

"We can take it on the picnic." I wished Josie had agreed to join us on the picnic. If she were here she'd do all the talking, but Josie said I'd do just fine by myself.

"May I help you?" Eleanor opened up the screen door and glared at Gray. In her stern black skirt and blouse

Eleanor looked like the boss of Sparrow Road. "This is private property."

"Sure." Gray kept one boot on the step, but I could see his shoulders shrink. "I'm here to visit Raine."

"Raine?" Eleanor looked at me. Then she glanced across the yard toward Viktor's office. "Where's your mother, Raine?"

"She's at our cottage."

She narrowed her beady eyes at Gray. "And how do you know Raine?" Eleanor jutted out her pointy chin.

Gray looked at me. "Well, I just do," he said. "I just know Raine."

"She's waiting for her father," Lillian said to Eleanor. "He has the means to feed her."

"Oh, stop with all that nonsense," Eleanor snapped at Lillian. "Raine, go get your mother now. And ask her to bring Viktor."

"No need for this," Gray said. "You're scaring Raine." Then he gave Eleanor a smile. "Heck, you're scaring me."

"Get your mother," Eleanor repeated. I jumped off the porch and ran. I didn't want Eleanor to do anything to Gray. I didn't want her to make Gray leave. There was the picnic, and Lillian's book of poetry I wanted Gray to read, and the most important mystery I hoped to solve today, the one Mama said Gray would have to tell me. Where did he disappear to all these years?

Mama came. She came racing up there barefoot still in her pajama shorts and T-shirt. She didn't say Gray was my father, but she said that he was safe. A friend of Viktor's who had permission to visit Sparrow Road.

"This man knows Raine?" Eleanor sneered.

"He does." Mama set her hand down on my head. "And you may go inside now, Eleanor. I'll take care of Raine."

"Well, someone should," Eleanor huffed. "This place! I came to write, but there's been nothing but distractions. Now I have to supervise someone else's child!" She let the screen door slam.

"I'm sure sorry I missed *her* at the barbecue," Gray joked.

Mama laughed a little. "Visitors," she said. "We don't get many at the house."

"I understand." Gray smiled at me. He had the kindest eyes I'd ever seen. "Like everybody, she's just watching out for Raine."

Gray and I decided to have our picnic at the lake. Just like the first night we went walking, we found little things to talk about, things that put us both at ease. I told him about meeting Nettie Johnson at the Blue Moon, and how she'd been an orphan. And Lillian's poem, the one she wrote for Viktor. Then I told about the attic. Lyman's drawing. The rows and rows of metal beds. How everything was left—jacks and dust and dirty socks.

"Quite a chapter for this place," Gray said. He grabbed a toothpick from his pocket. He told me he'd quit smoking seven weeks ago, and the toothpicks gave him something new to gnaw.

"Lillian was an orphan," I said. "At least I think she was."

Gray nodded, as if he wasn't real surprised. I wondered how much he and Viktor talked, how much Gray already knew about the orphanage. Gray seemed to be the only person in Comfort Viktor knew by name.

"Your mama sure can bake." He handed me a second pumpkin bar. "What about that poetry?"

I opened up to "February." "Here," I said. "This is the poem I mean. The one that I was puzzling over this morning when you came."

"You are a question I will carry," Gray drawled. Lillian's words sounded like a song. "Through Februaries far into my future." When he finished with the whole poem, he tilted back his head and let the sun soak his face. "I guess I got a sense of it," Gray said. "She'll be thinking long of somebody. Somebody she must have lost one February. And 'cause she lost them young, she didn't know how long the missing would go on. Lots and lots of winters." Gray sat up straight and stared at me. "I had the same hurt in October."

A wave of heat rushed up to my chest. My birthday was October 17. Gray was talking about me.

"You were my question, Raine." Gray chewed hard on the toothpick. "'Course I wondered lots of other days. But those Octobers, they reminded me the time was moving on. Year after year, they kept up like a clock. And all the years just added up. I guess those were my Februaries." Gray dropped his head into his hands. "I know you're waiting for a story."

"I am," I said. I'd been waiting since the day Mama told me who he was. Longer in my heart, but I didn't think I'd ever hear it. "Mama said you'd tell me it yourself. Where you've been. Why you never saw me. Why I didn't meet you until now."

"I know I owe it to you, Raine. Trouble is, I wish you knew me better first. The man I am today. Maybe see some good in me before I tell you all the bad." Across Sorrow Lake, a small fawn stood startled in place. "It's scared," Gray said. "Like me." Then suddenly it turned and darted toward the trees.

"Go ahead," I said. It was the same thing I told Mama. "Just start at the beginning."

I had a name now and a face, a man with timid deer eyes and my crooked wolf dog teeth, a man who sang slow songs, a short man with small shoulders. I had all that, but I still couldn't tell myself the story of my life.

"Well, you know Amsterdam," Gray said. "Your mama said she told you how we met. Outside of that cathedral. How she was singing on the street for extra cash. Coins people threw into her guitar case. And that day she'd gathered quite a crowd."

"Mama never mentioned a cathedral." When it came to Amsterdam, Mama left out most the details.

"No?" Gray said. "Well, it was quite a scene. Your mama barefoot, with those beautiful red curls. People packed together just to listen to her sing." Gray gave a little whistle. "And from the second that I saw her, heard her, your mama had my heart." Gray put his hand against his chest. "This probably just sounds silly to you now."

"No," I said. I had so little to hold on to that none of it seemed silly.

"You sure?" Gray said.

I liked to picture Mama that first day, a young girl singing on the street, while Gray James slouched along the sidelines, already in love.

Gray tugged his tie loose, yanked it free, and set it on the blanket. "That kind of love, it happens in a snap. Happens without thinking of the troubles up ahead. And I was there on tour with my first album, just a greenhorn from Missouri. So young, I didn't know Amsterdam from Spain." Gray gave my tennis shoe a squeeze. "Bored yet?"

"Nope," I said. "Keep going." So far I wasn't even born.

Gray rolled up his sleeves and propped his elbows on his knees. A butterfly landed on his boot. "Pretty place," Gray said. He watched the lake and waited like he was gathering up courage for a story about more than love and Mama's songs. "So anyway, time came I had to move on from Amsterdam. That's how it is with records, you travel place to place. Live out on the road. And your mama, she was drifting too. Living some in France and Spain. Neither of us even owned a phone. Or had a steady address to our names."

"You lost track of Mama?"

"More or less." He yanked a fist of grass and let it sift out through his fingers. "Making music didn't leave much time for love. And some time passed before I found her in Milwaukee. And by then—." Gray pulled a faded leather wallet from his jeans. "You were in the world."

"You found us in Milwaukee? Mama never told me that." All these years I could have known Gray.

"Here." Gray slid out a yellowed snapshot. "First time we got to meet."

I stared down at the picture. It was me back as a toddler; me held tight in Gray James's arms. Me, in that blue corduroy jacket with a bear patch on the chest. I still had it with my keepsakes. Beneath the photo in the border Gray had printed *Raine and me.*

"We met? Before the barbecue?" I wished I had one memory of Gray, one memory of us together in Milwaukee. I wished I had that snapshot for myself.

He nodded, then slid it back into his wallet. There didn't seem to be much in there besides us and a couple dollar bills. "That snapshot means the world to me."

"But what happened after that? Didn't you ever visit me again?"

"I did," Gray said. "Or I tried a couple times. But by then, your mama didn't much want me in your life." Gray took the toothpick from his teeth and snapped it straight in two. Then he stuck another in his mouth. "Thing is—" Gray dropped his head, let his shaggy bangs cover his eyes. "By then, I had a problem with my drinking. A big, big problem. I wasn't really fit to be a father."

"You drank?"

"I did." Gray kept his head hung. "So much, I wasn't worth much."

The only man I knew who had a problem with drinking was Mr. Earle, Tessa's horrible dad, who lived in 303. Mr. Earle, who staggered down our hallway. Mr. Earle, who passed out in a snowbank Christmas Eve and Grandpa Mac had to help him to his door. Mr. Earle, who hit Tessa in the head so hard it left a bruise over her eye. Once, in the middle of the night, I had to give my bed to Tessa and her mother because Mr. Earle was drunk. And the next day, Tessa and her mother moved away. Gone for good. With money Mama and Grandpa Mac had given them. And Mr. Earle was still drunk on our steps. Still mean. I always wished he'd been the one to go. "You drank?" My stomach turned. I didn't want a man like Mr. Earle to be my father.

"Sad to say," Gray said. "But the truth is that I did. And your mama only let me see you when I was sober. And back then, I wasn't sober all that much."

"Never?" I said. "Not in twelve whole years? You weren't ever sober on my birthday? Or Christmas? Or any ordinary day when you could have known me?"

"I wish I didn't have to tell this to you, Raine. But you're looking for an answer. And I know I got to tell the truth before we can move on."

I stared out at the lake. I wasn't sure I was moving on with Gray—not with a man who drank like Mr. Earle.

"The last time that I saw you," Gray said, "I was performing in Chicago and I drove up to your place. I was in good shape that day, good enough that your mama let me take you to the park. I had a dream to push you on the

swing. Listen to your stories. You sure could talk at three."
A quick smile lit up Gray's guilty face. Then he tore a
patch of grass down to the dirt.

"But going to the park that day, I saw a bottle in a
window. And I stopped into a store, bought something
that I shouldn't. I only meant to take a couple sips, but I
couldn't stop." Gray squeezed his eyes shut tight, like there
was something in the memory he couldn't bear. "Somehow
I passed out on a park bench."

"You passed out in a park? With me?"

He gave a sad, slow nod. "And I didn't wake until I
heard your mama screaming. Calling for you, Raine. But
by then, you were long gone."

"Gone?" This didn't seem like a story from my life.
Grandpa Mac and Mama had always kept me close. No
wonder Mama was afraid I'd disappear. "How long was I
missing?"

"Too long," Gray finally said. "No one's really sure. After
a while someone found you crying in an alley. Called up
the police. Of course, after that—" Gray hesitated, but he
didn't need to finish off his sentence. I knew what happened
after that. Mama would never want me to be with Gray
James again. "I hate this story, Raine. It's a shame I've had to
live with." Gray hung his head, but I didn't care. He should
have been ashamed. "I wish I had another truth to tell."

"And even so you kept up with the drinking? Even
though you lost me?" Somehow I had the answer in my

heart. If Gray had quit, I would have known him before now.

"After that, the drinking just got worse. There were days I hardly knew my name."

Blood thrummed in my ears. "You could've quit." A fire burned inside my throat.

"I tried." Gray frowned. "I did. Lots and lots of times. But trying isn't doing. And the music life I lived, singing place to place, there was always someone buying the next drink. It wasn't till last year—" He reached into the pocket of his shirt and pulled out a kind of coin, bronze, the size of a half dollar. "I finally woke up, Raine."

He pressed the metal coin into my palm. "It's not a fancy thing. But it's worth a lot to me. I earned it for one year without a drink." In the center of the coin was a circled number I. "One year," he said again. He pointed to some words written on the edge. "Shakespeare," he said. "'To thine own self be true.' And so I have to be. And true to you as well."

Gray's one-year coin didn't mean a thing to me. No one ever gave Mama or Grandpa Mac a medal for not drinking. Or for taking care of me. Gray should have given up the drinking, coin or not.

"It's late," Gray said. "I know that, Raine. And I'm sorry for all the bad that happened. All the years I've been away. Sorry for that day I lost you in the park. Let your mama down."

Yahoo. Maybe Grandpa Mac was right. I handed back the bronze medallion. Gray's drinking story only made the years I missed him worse. All that wonder, and Gray was getting drunk.

"No." He shook his head. "I earned it for you, Raine."

I dropped it in my pocket; I wanted Gray to leave. "I should go." I stood up and swept the dried grass from my jeans. Just those words made me almost cry.

"Raine," Gray said. "I'm finished with the drinking."

"Okay," I said. I picked up Mama's picnic basket and threw the checkered napkins in with all the garbage. I was ready for this Gray day to be done.

When Gray's van pulled out of the driveway, I didn't say a word to anybody. I dumped the picnic basket in the barn, grabbed my bike, and took off by myself. I didn't know where I was going. Part of me wanted to ride back to Milwaukee, to the girl I used to be. The Raine O'Rourke I was before I knew I had a father who loved drinking more than me.

I rode so far and fast my heart hurt. My father was so drunk he couldn't see me on my birthday, or send a card at Christmas, or go long enough without a drink to find out how I was.

When I got tired of riding, I dropped my bike into the weeds, let it fall so hard the fender bent against the wheel. I sat down in the field and cried all by myself. Far away from Sparrow Road, so no one else would see me. I pulled his bronze medallion from my pocket and set it down beside me. One year without a drink. Gray should have quit a long, long time ago.

I don't know how long I sat there, but when Viktor's truck skidded to a stop out on the gravel, I didn't want him to see my tear-streaked face.

"Raine!" Diego jumped down from the back end of the truck and waded through the tall grass like a bear. "Raine, are you okay?" He rested his warm hand against my head.

I hid my face between my knees. "I don't want to talk to Viktor," I mumbled through my legs.

"No," Diego said. "I understand." He gave my head a pat. "Raine's okay," he yelled to Viktor. "Let Molly know we found her. The two of us are on our way back home."

Diego crouched beside me in the grass. "Your mama's looking everywhere for you. She's got everybody searching." Maybe Mama was remembering the day Gray lost me in the park? "Even Eleanor."

"Eleanor was searching?" I couldn't imagine Eleanor looking anywhere for me.

Diego laughed. "It's that crazy mother instinct." It was good to hear his big roar fill the field.

"Gray drank," I said. I had to get it off my chest, even though it made me feel ashamed to come from a man that drank like Mr. Earle. "He drank and drank."

"I know," Diego said. "Your mama told me, Raine." He plucked a long, green weed and let a caterpillar inch off it toward my arm. "But the good news is, he's been sober since last summer. That's no small achievement, Raine. It's like climbing up a mountain every day. Drinking's not an easy thing to end." He nodded toward Gray's bronze medallion shining in the weeds. "It took a lot to earn that."

"He lost me at a park. A stranger found me crying in an alley." The last part made me choke up on new tears. "And he was too drunk to see me on my birthdays, or Christmas, or all the other days I wondered where he was."

"All terrible things," Diego said.

I let the caterpillar crawl across my skin, touched my fingers to its tiny hairs. Once, Mama hung a cocoon in our front window, but no butterfly ever burst out of the gauzy bubble. It was still hard for me to see how one thing grew out of the other.

"But for what it's worth—Gray's doing well today. And he only has today. And tomorrow, and whatever good he can do into the future."

I licked the salty tears off of my lips. I wanted to go home and splash cold water on my face.

"Your mama's done a hard, brave thing. She let Gray have a chance with you this summer, because in the end, she wants to do what's right. And your knowing Gray is right."

"But I was happy with Grandpa Mac and Mama." I knew now why Mama didn't want to lose the good life that we had.

"But you would have always wondered. And even with his troubles, Gray James is still your dad."

Your dad. Both times Diego said it the words seemed a plain, true fact. *Your dad.* Like a thing I couldn't change. Gray was my dad, whether he was the dad I wanted now or not. I let the caterpillar crawl back into the weeds. Then I picked up Gray's one-year medallion. I didn't want Diego to think I'd be mean enough to leave it.

"And pretty soon," Diego said, "this summer won't be summer anymore. We all ought to make the most of it, I think." He lifted up my bike and pulled the fender straight. "Your mama's waiting, Raine. Climb up on those handlebars, young lady. I'm going to take you home."

He held the old bike steady while I settled in the center, face forward, the metal handlebars hot inside my hands. "Hold tight," he said. We wobbled. We teetered and careened. "Fear not!" Diego yelled into the wind. "You're in good hands with me!"

Before we made it to the driveway, Mama scooped me off the handlebars and squeezed me to her chest. She was trembling so hard I felt like I was smothered in an earthquake. "I didn't know where you went or how I'd ever find you. You can't just leave Sparrow Road without a word."

"Molly, Raine is safe," Diego said. Then he left us standing there alone.

"Raine, I was so worried." Mama kissed my hair. I knew she was remembering that park and how Gray almost lost me. No wonder all these years Mama feared I'd disappear.

"I know about the drinking." Just saying it sent the tears back down my face. "And how Gray passed out in that park. And how he just couldn't quit. Not even to see me."

"Oh, Raine," Mama whispered. "I wish I could have given you the kind of dad that you deserve."

I thought of Tessa and her bruises. Mrs. Earle and Tessa sleeping in my bed. "Was Gray like Mr. Earle? Was he mean?"

"Mr. Earle?" Mama gasped. "Oh no! Gray's nothing like him, Raine."

"You're sure?" I reached into my pocket and brushed my fingers over Gray's medallion. "But did he drink like that back when you fell in love? In Amsterdam?"

"No," Mama said. "We were so young in Amsterdam, and Gray wasn't drinking then. He was shy. Sweet. Pretty much the way he is today. But the music life, the crowds, performing place to place—all of it took a toll on Gray."

"I wish he'd never changed," I said. "I wish he hadn't started drinking."

"Me too," Mama said. "I've wished that for so long."

When I woke up the next morning, a folded scrap of paper had been slid beneath our door. *R— Come see me bright and early in my shed. J.*

Before Mama got a glimpse, I tucked the note into my bag. She'd never let me visit Josie's shed. "I'm off to write," I said. It wasn't quite a lie.

"No breakfast?" Mama frowned.

"Nope," I said. Since yesterday with Gray, my stomach had felt too sad for food.

"Okay." Mama gave a worried smile. "But stay here on the grounds. No more sudden bike trips by yourself."

I kissed her on the cheek. "Don't worry. I won't leave Sparrow Road."

Inside Josie's shed smelled a little bit like Christmas, a mix of peppermint and pine. Cinnamon. It felt like dreams were floating in the air. Cloth scraps were scattered on the floor. Memory patches were tacked along the walls. Our root beer float. The two of us in our rowboat on the lake. A tiny velvet square of Lyman's snowy drawing. It seemed impossible that Josie could make a memory come alive on just a scrap of fabric. I wished I had my own quilt full of memories, so I could still have Sparrow Road years and years from now.

"Morning, Raine Cloud, grab a seat." Josie swept a clearing with her hand. She sat there in the center of the floor, her patchwork skirt bunched up around her knees, her big black boots thrown over in the corner.

"But Viktor?" Out the window, the meadow had the emptiness of morning. Still, I didn't want him to catch me in the shed.

"Hopefully asleep," Josie said. "I've never seen the Iceberg out this early."

I closed the door, turned the little lock. It felt like I was entering some kind of holy space, a little messy church full of someone else's dreams.

"How's the heart today?" Josie asked.

"So-so," I said. A kind of tear fog hung over my head. Mama said swallowing Gray's truth might take a little time. More than just a single night of sleep.

"I've been on a roll all night," Josie yawned. "I had to have some company before I lost my mind." On the floor, surrounded by the scraps, Josie looked like she'd already lost her mind. "I want to show you something."

She rummaged through a mound of fabric. "Shoot," she said. "I thought it was right here." Josie's shed was messier than my bedroom in Milwaukee. "Eureka!" She pulled a hand-stitched doll out of the scraps and handed it to me. "Look! It's my own brilliant invention. The Eureka Doll."

The Eureka Doll was the size of Josie's giant hand, maybe a little bigger; her face was blank, her body made from little fabric odds and ends. Patchwork, like most of Josie's things. "Patent pending." Josie gave me her widest gap-toothed grin. "Want to know the magic?"

"Sure," I said. I could tell this doll was another one of Josie crazy schemes.

"You put a question in its belly, and while you're sewing, while you're bringing your Eureka Doll to life, your answer will suddenly appear. Eureka!" Josie shouted. "Which really means aha!"

I squeezed the spongy stomach; I couldn't feel a question. "What'd you ask this one?"

Josie shrugged. "That's the beauty of it. After a while, even the question disappears. I swear this to you, Raine." Josie made an X across her chest. "In Detroit, I've got an entire group of wayward kids who all sew these after school." Someday I wanted to see Josie with the tough kids she taught.

"So how long does it take?"

"Oh," Josie said. "You never know. You just sew and sew and suddenly an answer will appear. A couple days. A week. Could be longer. All these tiny scraps take time." She passed a sewing basket overflowing with supplies. "Want to give the doll a try while we hang out?"

"I don't have a question," I said. "At least not one the Eureka Doll could answer."

Josie grinned. "One will come. Just grab some scraps, choose fabrics that you like."

I cut the body from a paper pattern Josie gave me. The starting out was easy; I could sew it with the simple stitches Mama taught me back when we used to make clothes for my dolls. "Just don't sew it closed," she warned. "You need space for the stuffing. And for a question, when one pops into your brain."

We worked there in the quiet, Josie cutting large scraps of fabric into shapes I'd never seen. Not squares or circles or triangles, but wild puzzle pieces she must have imagined in her mind.

"Is that your piece for the Arts Extravaganza?" I asked.

Josie said we'd all have artwork to show the people at our party, but Josie's project looked like a big velvet sheet with blobs. And I still wasn't sure what my art would be; Lyman's story was mostly bits and pieces. Nothing I could show.

"It is," she said. "Don't worry, Raine. The worse the mess, the more I get to wonder."

I poked the needle through the fabric, stitched another scrap. There was a kind of steady rhythm to the sewing that gave me time to think. I thought of Gray. I thought of yesterday, the way he'd stood slump shouldered in the driveway, a toothpick in his teeth, looking like he'd let me down in more ways than he could count.

When he finally said, "I'll see ya?" he said it like a question, like he was waiting for a yes or no from me. I didn't know what to tell him, so I turned and walked away.

I'll see ya? Was that a question I could sew into a stomach? "Can it be someone else's question?" I asked Josie.

"You bet," she said. "No rules. The doll is yours; you own it, heart and soul."

I looked down into my doll's blank face. Her body was a scrap of worn bedsheet.

I'll see ya? I printed on a scrap of old white felt. When my doll was nearly finished, I'd stick it in her stomach, the same place Gray's final question was sitting hard in me.

"So," Josie said. "I need your help here, Raine." She stared up at the sheet. "I keep dwelling on those orphans." She pinned a paisley curl onto the velvet. "And I keep thinking about poor Nettie Johnson's story. How long she waited for her dad to come back from the army."

"Long," I said. I couldn't imagine watching from that broken attic window for Gray James to walk over those hills. Sometimes when I was little, I used to wonder about strange men I walked by on the street. But it wasn't the kind of lonely wait an orphan would have had. *"A kind of lonely that won't go,"* I said. "That's a line from one of Gray's sad songs."

"That's it. A lonely that won't go," Josie said. She pinned up another scrap of fabric. "But here's what I don't know. Do you think those orphans were better off without their parents? I mean, what if Nettie Johnson's dad hadn't been the dad she dreamed?" Josie stretched a long black ribbon down the center, then moved it to the side.

"If she comes to the Arts Extravaganza you can ask her." I didn't get the feeling we'd see Nettie Johnson before that.

"But that will be too late." Josie pulled another straight pin from her pocket. "I need it for this piece. I need to know what emotion to convey. What the orphans felt living in that attic. I can't tell if it's longing or relief. Because maybe being an orphan was better than being with bad parents? Parents who were too poor or sick or mixed up to take care of their kids?"

I thought of Lyman and his drawing; how I imagined he felt a lot like me. How he looked into the mirror to see his father's face. I knew what he would say. "No," I said. "No matter what, those kids still wanted their parents."

"You know," Josie sighed. "That's exactly what I think."

35

"I always dreamed of my own doll," Lillian said, running her hand over the fabric. Sometimes instead of reading I just sat with her and sewed. Three days had passed since Gray had left me with his question, and bit by bit the scraps were turning to a doll. I still didn't have an answer, but the steady act of sewing gave my heart some peace.

"We can make one for you when I'm finished," I offered. "Or I'll sew you one myself."

"Really?" Lillian's face lit up. "You could sew a doll for me?"

"Sure," I said. "I'll ask Josie to bring a box of scraps up from her shed. You can pick out your own colors." I knew Josie would want Lillian to have a doll to keep.

Lillian stroked my cheek. "You've made Sparrow Road your home."

"Home?" I said.

"You've settled in. Made up your mind to stay. Stopped waiting. I can always tell when the new children reach that point. If you'd like, we could begin your piano lessons; it seems to me you're ready for those now."

"Okay," I said. "But there isn't a piano in the house."

"Perhaps you should ask Viktor. He's in charge of music lessons now. You know, he is a genius. A child prodigy. I saw that from the start. The Berglunds plan to send him to Austria to study." Lillian made a little frown. "I'm afraid that's far away for a young boy."

"Did Viktor live here, Lillian?" I thought about his symphonies, the way they sounded more like suffering than songs. The gingerbread he said Lillian baked each Christmas. All those nights he sat beside her on the porch. The way he let her break the silence rule with me. "When you used to teach piano?"

"Viktor is a Berglund." Lillian stared down at her hands.

"But why was he the question that you carried? The question that you carried *so far into the future*?" It was Lillian's poem that started Gray on telling me his story, but in all that talk of drinking I'd forgotten what he said about the poem. Something about lots of years of missing someone gone. "The one you dedicated to V."

Lillian lifted her face like she was rising out of water. "Yes," she said. "No matter what, we miss the ones we love."

I still don't have an answer to Gray's question, I wrote Lyman. I was upstairs with a flashlight and my sketchbook, writing before I fell asleep. Outside Mama and Diego were talking on our swing. My Eureka Doll was nearly done; tomorrow I'd stuff her full of batting, slip the question in, and finish the last stitch. *Nothing*, I said. *I still don't know what to say to Gray's "I'll see ya?"*

Lyman smiled. He was standing at my window, staring at the moon. *I never heard of an answer coming from a doll.*

No, I said. *Me either. But somehow all of Josie's crazy notions seem to happen.*

But if it did, Lyman said, *I know the question I'd stuff into the stomach.*

What? I asked.

Why didn't you ever find me?

Your dad? I asked.

Yep, Lyman said. *'Cause drinking or no drinking, you're lucky yours found you.*

It was the next day, underneath the willow with nothing but the silence, that I opened up my sketchbook and wrote my thoughts to Gray. First, I wrote down all the mad and sad and letdown that weighed heavy on my heart. I started with all the things Gray missed: every single birthday, my first communion, ice-skating, sledding, the father-daughter Girl Scout breakfasts, father-daughter camping, the science fair, the ribbons that I won on field day, school concerts, every Christmas, every Easter, every Halloween he didn't see me in my costumes or go with me trick or treating.

He never tucked me into bed at night or waited mornings while I got on the bus. I said I couldn't forgive him for the day he got so drunk I ended up with the police. And that he looked too happy on that album with his beer and cigarette, and that after twelve long years of nothing it was late for him to want to know me now. I wrote it all and then I ripped it up.

When I started a fresh page, I didn't know what more I had to say until I said it. I only knew I still had other feelings pressing on my heart.

Gray, I wrote because no matter what, I couldn't start out with *Dear.*

All the days since we went out on the picnic, I've been thinking of the things I want to say, things that were going through my mind while I listened to your story, things I couldn't say that day because I didn't even have the words. I was too full of shock and sad and mad and mostly disappointment.

Here's what I can say, just so you understand.

Twelve years was a long, long time to wait. Time that left me free to dream a lot of things. Good and bad. But none of them were the story that you told me. I never dreamed you were off drinking, or that you lost me in Milwaukee at a park. Or that a stranger found me crying in an alley. Or that, year after year, you picked drinking instead of seeing me. All that truth was hard to hear, even if I asked for it. And it's still hard after all these days, but I guess the truth is part of growing up. Part of knowing what was or used to be. And at least I don't have to wonder anymore.

And it's good you gave up drinking, good you made it up that mountain. Good you made it one whole year so we could finally meet. (I'm not going to count the times I can't remember.) And I'm glad Mama brought us here to let you have a chance with me. I am. Even if it's harder than I thought.

So if you're really done with all the drinking, I think I can still see you while we're here. A couple times at least. Before summer isn't summer anymore. And all my days at Sparrow Road are gone. And we go back to Milwaukee. Because who knows what will happen then.

I hope you plan to play at the Arts Extravaganza. Josie has her heart set on your music. And I'd really like to hear you sing one of those sad songs for myself.

See you soon then,

Raine

I picked up my needle and looped in the last stitches. I had my answer to Gray's *See ya?* and my Eureka Doll was done.

36

I didn't see Gray right away; we started with small notes Viktor carried back and forth between us. I told about my piano lessons, how Viktor let Lillian teach me in the old infirmary, and how I learned to play simple songs like "Twinkle, Twinkle" on Viktor's grand piano, with his scribbled sheets of music scattered on the floor. I wrote about the Arts Extravaganza—the plans I made with Josie. The games we both invented. The food we hoped to serve. I even wrote about the pineapple upside-down cake I'd baked Diego for his birthday.

Mostly the notes that Gray sent me were a bunch of ways of saying he was sorry. Sorry for the years he didn't come for my birthdays. The twelve good years he wasted. The terrible day he lost me in the park. Plus everything I listed in the letter, and lots more that Gray dreamed up. I didn't need all of his apologies, but Diego said Gray did. Diego said asking for forgiveness was Gray's way of getting well.

When I finally did see Gray it was at the Comfort Kitchen. Mama said she'd rather he come back for a picnic or a visit to our cottage, but this time I wanted to meet Gray on my own. Someplace far away from our last bad conversation. A place where we could get a brand-new start.

"Okay, Raine," Josie said when Gray walked into the restaurant for our lunch. "Two thirty at the five-and-dime." Josie promised Mama she'd bike with me both ways. "You two enjoy your eats! The Arts Extravaganza calls!" Josie's hands were full of bright green fliers she was passing out to strangers.

"You're sure busy with that party," Gray said as we slid into a booth.

"Lillian and I are picking out her poems. And we've got days of baking up ahead." We still had to bake and freeze fourteen dozen cookies—peanut butter, oatmeal raisin, chocolate chip—and at least ten pans of Mama's caramel brownies. Diego was in charge of sloppy joes. Even awful Eleanor was reading from her essays. I still wasn't sure what my art would be. Mama didn't know what her art would be yet either, but every day I begged her to play that old guitar. I wanted everyone to see the girl she used to be, the singer she still was. "Everyone is helping with the party."

"Nice folks at that place." Gray laid his paper napkin on his lap. "They sure do like you, Raine."

"Not everyone," I said. "Not Eleanor. Or Viktor."

"Aw," Gray said. "I wouldn't be so sure about Viktor. Some men keep their hearts hid pretty deep."

"Do you?" I asked.

"Heck no." Gray gave his little laugh. "I can't keep my heart hid much at all."

It was easier to meet Gray in a restaurant with the solid wooden table set between us, and the customers, and the waitress, Dot, stopping by to pour fresh coffee in Gray's cup. Dot knew Gray by name, knew his order without Gray even asking. Gray said all his suppers were spent here.

"Your Grandpa Mac still plan on coming?" Gray rubbed his hand against his jaw.

"He said he would." I munched a bite of a sweet potato fry. Sweet potato fries were Gray's favorite food in Comfort. "I'm sure he's going to come." When I'd called Grandpa Mac to ask him, he said wild horses couldn't keep him away.

I still hadn't told Grandpa Mac that I'd met Gray, or that I knew about the drinking or the day Gray lost me in the park. That was something I wanted to tell him face-to-face, so he could see I was safe. Safe and sound. Even with Gray's truth.

Gray rubbed his jaw again. "You know, that day I lost you at the park?" He hung his head like all those apologies he sent hadn't helped his shame. "Your Grandpa Mac, he punched me in the face. Nearly broke my jaw. For months I couldn't sing straight. Though I know I did deserve it."

"Grandpa Mac punched you?" I knew Grandpa Mac had been some kind of boxer in the navy, but I never saw him lift his fist to anyone in anger. Grandpa Mac raised Mama without spankings. Same way they raised me. The O'Rourkes just never hit.

"Oh, he definitely did. I'm only telling you this 'cause I don't want to spoil your party. Your Grandpa Mac won't want to see me there. And he sure won't want to hear me sing. You'll have a better party with me gone."

"No," I said. I stuck my long spoon into my shake. "It'll be okay." I wanted all of them at the Arts Extravaganza—Gray and Grandpa Mac and Mama—but most of all I wanted our family troubles to be done.

After lunch was finished, the two of us took a slow walk down the shady streets of Comfort. When we reached the Soap-N-Sudz, Gray pointed to his place, a single rented room above a Laundromat. "Didn't you make a lot of money playing music?" I asked.

"Just enough to get me into trouble." Gray's bangs hung over his black eyes. "But some of it, I've saved in your name." Gray moved the toothpick with his teeth.

"My name?"

"Yep." Gray put his hands in his back pocket. "At Summit Bank there in Milwaukee. There's money for your mama too, but she won't take it. Never would. But in the end, I know money don't mean much. I know it can't make up for my mistakes. Or all the time I missed."

"No," I said. I didn't want Gray's money either. "But it was nice you kept us in your mind; thought of us at least."

"Oh. I sure did, Raine." Gray's shy face lightened up a little. "I thought and thought."

"Me too," I said. "But now I'm glad those mysteries are done."

Gray left me outside the Soap-N-Sudz while he went up for Mr. Bones. He said his place was too lowdown for company. It was a stopping-for-a-short-stay kind of place. A bridge between where he was and where he thought he ought to be. Not so far from the trailer in Missouri where he started.

When he stepped outside, Gray had Mr. Bones cradled in his arms. Mr. Bones was half the size of Beauty, with a bony spine that ran like a lumpy path straight down his skinny back. "I don't let him loose," Gray said. "Wouldn't want him to get lost."

"You sound just like Mama." I laughed. "It's the same way she treats me."

"Sure," Gray said. "I guess too much love is like that."

He petted Mr. Bones behind the ears; together they made the perfect misfit pair. I wished I had a camera so I could save Gray in this minute.

"Uh-oh," Gray said when Mr. Bones began to wiggle. We stepped inside the shadowed stairwell, shut the metal door, and sat down on the grimy steps so Gray could let him free. "He sure does like you, Raine," Gray said when Mr. Bones curled up on my lap. It made me sad to think of Gray climbing those dirty stairs alone, eating the same supper at the Comfort Kitchen every night.

"Why'd you come to Comfort in the first place?" I asked. "And how do you know Viktor?" There were still pieces to Gray's puzzle I hadn't put together.

"Oh," Gray said. "I thought we might go without my troubles for one day. Just have the here and now."

"We have the here and now," I said. Mr. Bones ran his scratchy tongue along my finger. "But I still want to hear it."

"It's long," Gray said. "We got to meet up with Josie by two thirty. I don't want your mama to worry if you're late."

"Just give me the abbreviated version," I said. "Paraphrase."

"Paraphrase?" Gray laughed. "You really are a wonder to me, Raine."

I sat there on those steps with Mr. Bones purring on my lap and listened to Gray's story. He said he'd come here for a place called New Connections, a place not too far from Comfort, a place for men like him who never could quit drinking on their own.

"And after I was finished," Gray said, "Viktor came out to New Connections, offered me a home, a job out at his place. Not really for the money, just steady work to keep me far from trouble. I'm not the only soul he's rescued, Raine. Viktor's helped a lot of down-and-outs. Folks hoping for a hand."

"Did you live at Sparrow Road?"

"I did," he said. "That old house needs a lot of help. I joined on with his work crew through that winter. Painted. Plastered. Anyway, it's how Viktor came to know I had a daughter. One I'd lost because of drinking. And somehow, without me knowing, he got your mama on the phone, told her I was sober, and talked her into meeting me for coffee in Milwaukee. It was Viktor who drove me to that meeting, and he sat right there beside me while your mama showed me pictures of you, Raine. All the years I'd missed. It made me know the family I'd let go." A hint of tears washed over Gray's black eyes. "Then Viktor offered her the cottage, so she could come this summer and see me for herself; see that my drinking days were really done. And maybe let me have a chance with you after all."

"That's how Mama got the job?"

"Yep," Gray said. "But it wasn't a job that Viktor offered. Your mama could have stayed at Sparrow Road for free. But your mama won't take charity. So Viktor said he'd hire her for whatever work she wanted. His housekeeper was moving off to Fargo at the end of June. Still, it took more months of convincing. More trips Viktor made to Milwaukee by himself. Trips without me knowing. I couldn't believe the day he drove over to my place and told me your mama had said yes. The two of you were coming here that week." Gray shook his head. "It was an all-out miracle for me."

"Viktor did all that so we could meet?" Suddenly, he wasn't just the Iceberg anymore.

"Silent as he seems, Viktor's life is mostly helping others. Not just me. Or the artists he offers his house to every summer. He's a man who lives to help. I suppose it's how he quiets his own troubles."

"Troubles?"

"Sure." Gray stretched out his legs. "Like the rest of us, I imagine Viktor's had his share."

"Have you ever heard his music?" I put my hands over my ears. "It sounds like children hurt."

"I have indeed," Gray said. "I never knew an instrument could make that kind of sound."

I ran my finger along Mr. Bones's soft neck. "Do you think Viktor might have been an orphan? Before he was a Berglund?"

"To tell the truth," Gray said, "that very thought has crossed my mind."

"It has?" I smiled. Gray James was a dreamer just like me.

When I got back to our cottage, I heard the little pluck of strings float out our bedroom window. And then I heard the hum of Mama's voice, followed by a few high *la-la-las*. Then some words about a river, and I knew Mama was upstairs in our bedroom playing that guitar. Mama hadn't touched it since the night Gray gave it to her as a gift.

I waited silent at the door so Mama wouldn't stop singing. Most of it was just the sound of songs that couldn't get started—Mama's fingers plucking at the strings—she'd play a few sweet notes and then she'd stop. It was a sound I'd waited lots of years to hear, not just Mama singing, but Mama playing a guitar. The way she did in all our old-time pictures.

Mama's fingers on those strings and her beautiful smooth voice reminded me of something I must have known once and then forgotten. A long-lost feeling, maybe my baby days in Amsterdam. Me on Mama's back, or Mama barefoot singing on the streets.

Upstairs Mama's voice skipped like a rock across the water. It rang beautiful and clear, pure and green. I knew why Gray had stopped to listen that first day in Amsterdam. And how Mama owned his heart.

I waited until the music finally stopped, until I heard Mama set the guitar back in the case and snap the latches shut.

"Mama," I called up to our bedroom.

"I'm up here, Raine." She was sitting on the bed, the guitar case right beside her. "How'd things go this time with Gray?" I saw the old fear in her eyes.

"Good," I said. "Lots better." I didn't want Mama to worry about Gray. Or me. I wanted the little time we had left here to be happy. "I heard you play."

"You did?" Mama hung her head. "I can't play anymore." Once Grandpa Mac said Mama threw away her future living like a hippie.

"You sure can. I heard you play and sing. And it was beautiful. It really, really was."

"I wish Gray hadn't given this to me," Mama said. She shoved the case away. "I've forgotten how to play. Some of it comes back, but most of it is gone." Then she opened up her arms for a huge hug. "But anyway, you're my music now."

"You could play that song you were just singing for our party. Let everybody hear it. Grandpa Mac and Gray."

"No," Mama said. Then she wrinkled up her forehead.

"Grandpa Mac and Gray. There's a frightening thought. I don't even know how Grandpa Mac will be with me. I'm sure he's still mad we even came to Sparrow Road."

"Mama." I sat beside her on the bed and dropped my cheek against her shoulder. "When Grandpa Mac gets here for the party, I want things to be okay."

"Okay?" Mama said. "Okay in what way, Raine?"

"The way they were before we left Milwaukee. All those years before Grandpa Mac got mad about this job. He wasn't mad at you, Mama, he was worried about Gray."

"I know." Mama pushed a curl back from her face. "But he should have trusted me. I wasn't going to put you in harm's way. I wasn't going to take a chance if Gray's drinking days weren't done. And you're my daughter, Raine. In the end, it's up to me to do what's best. Not Grandpa Mac. I can't stay his little girl forever."

"You're right." I smiled at Mama. "Just like I can't stay yours."

Mama kissed me on the forehead. "I'm learning that too, Raine."

"I just want the Arts Extravaganza to be happy. Everybody. My family. And all the people who come to Sparrow Road. Even Nettie Johnson, when she sees this place again."

"Nettie Johnson?" Mama said.

"The woman Josie and I met for pie that day. The one who was an orphan here."

"Do you think she's really coming?" Mama asked.

"I hope," I said. "I hope everybody comes. And when they do, I want it all to be pure happy. I want Grandpa Mac to see our time here wasn't a mistake. And for him to give Gray a second chance. Because I did."

"Whoa!" Mama laughed. "That's quite a list. I'm afraid you're getting as headstrong as dear Josie." She lifted up my chin. "I'll try to make my peace with Grandpa Mac, but I wouldn't hold out much hope for Grandpa Mac and Gray. Grandpa Mac's not one to let go of a grudge."

"He can do it for the party," I said.

"Well," Mama sighed, "we'll see."

Preparations for the Arts Extravaganza gave a new hum to the house. Mama and I baked so many bars and cookies the freezer was stocked full. Lillian cut linen squares for napkins; Diego scrubbed the floors. Josie spent hours in the barn fixing broken chairs and tables, digging out boxes of old dishes, silverware, crystal trays, things she said we'd need to serve the guests. Even Gray stopped by one day to string Christmas lights through trees.

Busy as we were, it still seemed to be forever before Grandpa Mac would get to Sparrow Road. Mama said his visit would come sooner if I quit counting down the days. But all that I could picture was Grandpa Mac in his big Buick pulling into our long driveway and the shocked look on his face when he saw Sparrow Road. The sprawling artists' house, the sky-high tower, the miles of rolling hills.

"You here, Josie?" I called into the barn. Lately all the party work kept us both too busy for our nightly sojourn to the attic. I missed sitting there with Josie and dreaming

Lyman's story, all the orphans' stories, thinking of *what was or what could be.*

"Buried under treasures," Josie called.

Even though hay and horses were long gone from the barn, I could still smell the old life in the wood. Mice darted between boxes. Birds nested in the rafters. Of all the buildings at Sparrow Road, I liked the barn the least. It reeked of mold and mildew, and it was filled with things left too long to rot. School desks and lamps and chests, blackboards, broken bikes, baseball bats and mitts, metal cribs, an old wheelchair pushed back in the corner, a black upright piano covered with thick cobwebs. And around it all, boxes stacked on boxes that Josie said were filled with years of life. It was Josie's favorite treasure-hunting place.

"This barn is amazing," Josie said. Her patchwork dress was smudged with streaks of dirt. "I could spend a year just searching."

She pointed to an old piano. "A little out of tune, but it still works. Try it out, I'd love to hear a song." So far all the songs that Lillian had taught me were little kids' songs. Nursery rhymes to music.

"We're not to 'Happy Birthday' yet," I said. I'd promised Josie that as soon as I learned "Happy Birthday" she could hear me play.

"Here!" She handed me a suitcase, child-sized, brown and battered at the edges, with a little leather handle and a sticker that said Austria peeled back on the front. "It's a stash of music. You can use it when you're finally done with that kid book Viktor found." I was learning from an old piano book that once belonged to Viktor, with the silver stars he earned for every perfect lesson still stuck on the page. It was hard for me to think a prodigy once learned songs that simple.

I snapped the metal latches open; inside a stack of old piano books was piled to the top. *Teaching Little Fingers. Ten Christmas Tunes. Songs for Happy Children.* None of these looked much better than playing "Twinkle, Twinkle." "I bet these were Lillian's," I said. "She probably used them for her lessons." I picked up *Ten Christmas Tunes*; maybe Lillian could teach me "Silent Night" before the summer ended.

A folded piece of paper fell out on my lap. Yellowed. With a single penny taped down on the front. Inside, the writing was from a kid in first or second grade. The kind of perfect printing Mrs. Swanson made us practice.

Dear Miss Hobbs,
This penny is for you. You gave it to me, but I don't want to keep it. I'd rather leave the luck with you and Lyman. I wish it wasn't only me who had a family now. I left a marble under Lyman's pillow. No matter how far away I have to go, I'll still miss Sparrow Road. Tell Lyman the same thing. I hope you won't forget me. Or all the songs you taught me. I know I never will.

I turned the paper over. No name. Not anywhere. I thought about that penny sitting on the attic floor, the one Diego found that first day that we met. A penny didn't seem worth much, but maybe it was then.

"What's that?" Josie looked up from her sorting. She had old tin cups hooked from every finger.

"A note that someone left. A child. Someone who loved Lillian."

"I have the feeling that they all did," Josie said. "Just the same as us."

It was the day before our party when I woke up with the sun. While Mama was asleep, I snuck out of our cottage, tiptoed through the main house, and went up the servants' staircase. I crept down the shadowed hallway. Josie's door was open, her bed was made, but Josie wasn't there. I crossed the hall and knocked on Diego's bedroom door.

"Raine?" he said, surprised. He stood there in the doorway, his wide face creased with sleep, his striped bathrobe knotted closed over his stomach. "Is something wrong?"

"Josie's gone already," I said. "I thought that you could help me."

"Of course," he yawned. "What is it you need?"

"Just someone to open up the attic."

"The attic?" Diego looked confused.

"The key's up on the ledge," I said. "It's too high for me to reach."

"The key?" Diego yawned again. "Is it even morning yet?" Except for us, the artists' house was silent.

"Sort of," I said. "But Grandpa Mac will be here this afternoon. And the party is tomorrow. And I still don't have any art to show."

"No?" Diego rubbed his sleepy eyes. "I wouldn't worry too much, Raine."

"But I want something there to show." Most of all I wanted a story to go with Lyman's drawing, a story that would capture all the things I imagined Lyman felt. What it was like to be an orphan in the attic, a boy who had a marble left beneath his pillow. But so far nothing that I wrote seemed to get it right. I needed to go up and sit still in the silence. Wait. Hope Lyman's words would come.

"You've been writing words for weeks," Diego said. "Just pick a piece closest to your heart. That's all art really is. Your feelings sent out to someone else." He pulled the silver key off of the ledge and unlocked the attic door.

"The trouble is—I need this to be *good*. Good enough for other folks to see. Not just my dreams. And nothing that I wrote yet really works."

"Ah," Diego yawned again. "*Good* will goof you up from the beginning. Art just has to be. Dream your dreams. Trust the words that come."

"I'll try," I said. And then I closed the door.

It was hours after I'd come down from the attic, hours after Mama had gone to town for groceries, and all of us had done a thousand things to get ready for the party, that

Grandpa Mac finally pulled into our driveway, got out of his big Buick, and wrapped me in his arms.

"Raine, Raine, Raine, Raine, Raine," he said. He hugged me so hard my feet flew off the ground; he must have kissed my head a hundred times. "I've never been so glad to get somewhere." He smelled like I remembered—spearmint gum and Irish Spring and coffee. "This has to be the longest trip I've ever taken." He let me down, then squished my cheeks between his hands. "Well, look at you!" He stared hard at my face. "I want to make sure you're the same girl that left me in Milwaukee."

"You look the same," I said. He was still big bellied like Diego, his gray hair shaved into short bristles. I squeezed his big warm hand; I was glad to have his great strength close again.

"This must be the welcome wagon," Grandpa Mac said. Everyone was lined up on the porch, Mama and the artists, even Eleanor. Lillian leaned on Viktor's arm.

"Grandpa Mac!" Josie shouted. "We're so thrilled you're finally here!" She bounded down the stairs, her patchwork dress waving in the rush. I was glad Grandpa Mac knew about the boots, the neon braids, Josie's wild ways. He didn't look surprised at all.

"Josie, yes?" he said. He gave her hand a giant shake. "Mac'll do the trick. I'm only Grandpa Mac to Raine."

Josie and I pulled him toward the porch. I wanted Mama

to rush right down the stairs with a giant hello hug, but instead she just stood quiet.

"Molly," Grandpa Mac called. "How you doing, honey?" It used to be Mama didn't come or go without a quick kiss on Grandpa's cheek.

"Dad," she finally said. She walked down the steps and gave Grandpa Mac a careful hug.

"Mama." I raised my eyebrows at her. If Mama couldn't be kinder, our family troubles wouldn't be better before the Arts Extravaganza.

"Did you find the place okay?" Her stiff voice softened some.

"No problem there." Grandpa Mac laughed. "I just followed all the flags." Josie and Diego had hung bright flapping flags all the way from the house out to the highway.

Grandpa Mac slung his arm over Mama's shoulder, and the three of us walked behind Josie to the house.

"Let me guess," Grandpa Mac said. He shook everybody's hand and knew them all by name. Lillian, Viktor, Eleanor, Diego. "Raine writes quite the letters," Grandpa Mac said. "I've had the play-by-play. She's sure loved her time at Sparrow Road."

"It certainly would seem so." Eleanor wrapped her arms around her stomach. "She's been a busy child." I wanted Eleanor to go back to her essays. I tugged on Grandpa Mac;

there was too much happy to let Eleanor put a cloud over my day. Mama's distant friendly worried me enough.

"Come on," I begged. "I want to show you everything."

"Raine," Mama scolded. "Grandpa Mac is probably tired. You should let him catch his breath."

"Don't worry about me, Molly," Grandpa Mac said. "I haven't felt this good for weeks!"

I gave Grandpa Mac the tour Viktor gave us our first day. We started with the meadow, the steep path to Sorrow Lake, the rowboat, the dock where Mama and I sunned. Then I walked him past the artists' sheds, showed him Viktor's turtles floating in their pond. Mama's fancy flower gardens. The infirmary. The barn. At every spot he listened to my stories, and then he added what he remembered from the letters—the Comfort Cone, Lillian's poems, my night swims with Josie and Diego.

He looped his arm around my shoulder and gave me a big squeeze. "Your letters sure do paint a picture."

"There's still our cottage and the attic, the tower, the servants' staircase, the library where I get Lillian's books. And before you leave, I'm going to take you on a rowboat ride. Just us all by ourselves."

"Oh my!" Grandpa Mac sighed. "I haven't seen you in so long. Could we take a minute to just sit?" Grandpa Mac's steps seemed too slow and hobbled. As much as I loved Lillian, I didn't want Grandpa Mac to grow that old.

"Okay," I said. "We'll rest."

I led him to the bench beneath the willow where I first heard Lyman speak. I'd told Grandpa Mac about most of Sparrow Road, except for Gray and Lyman. Lyman, because imagination and *what if* and *what was or what could be* was too confusing to tell Grandpa Mac long distance. And Gray? Because first Grandpa Mac had to see that I was safe. See that I could be okay with Gray James in my life.

"This place is really something, Raine." Grandpa Mac wiped his face off with his sleeve. "I see it's got a few legs up on old Milwaukee."

"I like the way the hills roll most of all. And how far you can see into the distance."

"It's nothing like the city, that's for sure."

I leaned in against Grandpa Mac's damp shirt. It seemed so strange to have him here at Sparrow Road. "I have more freedom here."

"I guess we kept you on a pretty short leash. I suppose you won't be in a hurry to come home?"

I sat quiet. There wasn't a good answer I could give. I wanted to go home to Grandpa Mac, but I didn't want Sparrow Road to end. I wanted Diego and Lillian and Josie and Gray and Lyman and these green fields and everything I'd come to love. Maybe that's why the orphan said he'd still miss Sparrow Road. Even with a family. I'd ask Lyman that this week.

"Grandpa Mac." I looked up so I could see him face-to-face. "I met Gray."

Grandpa Mac didn't blink or smile or frown, he kept his face completely straight and steady. "I expected that you would, Raine. It's what your mama wanted."

"Not Mama," I said. "It's what I wanted. Mama left it up to me."

"So?" He raised his bushy eyebrows. "You make it through okay?"

I nodded. "Gray's been sober for a year now. I know about his drinking."

Grandpa Mac clicked his tongue against his teeth. "I'm not sure you had to know about that, Raine. Those are grown-up problems."

"I'm old enough to know it, Grandpa Mac. And kids are always part of grown-up problems. Even when the grown-ups think they aren't."

"Maybe so." Grandpa Mac stared at me. "Though it'd be better if they weren't."

"I'm glad that I met Gray. I really am." I grabbed Grandpa Mac's warm hand. "I really, really am. And I look a little like him, my dark eyes. I have his teeth. And I'm small like him." I wanted Grandpa Mac to know Gray James was part of me.

"The O'Rourkes aren't exactly giants," Grandpa Mac said. "And my mother had brown eyes."

"Grandpa Mac." I gave his hand a squeeze. "Gray James is my dad." The second that I said it, tears came and Grandpa Mac's eyes clouded up with mine. I knew it hurt him just to hear it. It hurt me worse to say it, because Grandpa Mac had been more dad to me than Gray. For twelve good years. But none of that would change. "And tomorrow when you meet him at the Arts Extravaganza, I don't want you to punch him in the face."

Grandpa Mac frowned. "Did Gray tell you that?"

"He did," I said. "And I know about the park. The day he drank and lost me."

"Oh no," Grandpa Mac growled. "He told you that? That's a horrible story, Raine."

"It was," I said. "But now I know the truth. And I don't think you should have hit him, Grandpa Mac."

"He's lucky he got off with just one punch—," Grandpa Mac started; then he stopped. "Okay, maybe I shouldn't have hit him quite so hard. But your mama did her best to keep you safe. We both did. And then that yahoo comes to town and—"

"I know," I said before Grandpa Mac got too worked up again. I could hear all of the old anger rising in his voice. "You did. And I'm safe. I am. It all worked out okay. And I just want to be a family now. Again. The way we used to be. You and me and Mama."

"We are," Grandpa Mac said.

"No," I said. "Not really. Not with you and Mama."

"No?" Grandpa Mac said.

"You need to say you're sorry."

"Sorry?" Grandpa Mac stiffened on the bench. "To whom? Not Gray James?"

"No," I said. "To Mama. You need to let her know she did the right thing coming here this summer. Letting me meet Gray."

He folded his big hands; Mama always told me sorry was a bitter pill for Grandpa Mac. "Okay." He tapped his thumbs together. "I'll do my best. But I'm not sure your mama wants my sorry. If her mind's made up already, I might as well say I'm sorry to the moon."

Early the next morning, Grandpa Mac's breakfast basket was waiting at our door. Painted eggs, fresh blueberries, and Josie's trademark golden glitter WELCOME. "Will you look at this?" Grandpa Mac held up his hand-stitched napkin. "G.M." He laughed. "That Josie's something else."

When Mama stumbled sleepy eyed downstairs, Grandpa Mac got up from the table and handed her a cup of steamy coffee. "You sleep okay, sweetheart? You stayed up awfully late working on that party." I'd forgotten Grandpa Mac watched and worried over Mama, just like she watched and worried over me.

"Not so late, Dad." Mama smiled at the welcome basket.

Grandpa Mac cradled Josie's egg. "I couldn't stand to crack a thing this pretty. I think I'll take mine back to Milwaukee, show the customers. They'd want to have a look."

"Sparrow Road won't seem real in Milwaukee," I said. "It'll be more like a dream."

"You might be right about that." Grandpa Mac set the

egg back in the basket. "Raine sure is lucky that she got a chance to live here, Molly."

"Really, Dad?" Mama said, surprised. "Is that what you *really* think?"

"It is," he said. "And you were right. Sparrow Road, the country, it was a good place for a child." I was so happy I wanted to jump up and knot my arms around his neck. It wasn't quite a sorry, but it was as close to an apology as Grandpa Mac would come.

The three of us were lounging in pajamas when Josie and Diego showed up at our door. "Josie's like a kid at Christmas," Diego moaned. "She won't even let me sleep. That's two days in a row I've been yanked out of my dreams." Diego gave me a quick wink. "Doesn't anybody sleep past sunrise anymore?"

"Sleep?" Josie threw her arms up toward the sky. "Who can sleep?" She was so wide awake it looked like she couldn't stay put in her own skin. "We get to see Diego's art this morning! And after all these months locked up in my shed, I get to show you mine. Come on."

"In our pajamas?" Mama said. "I haven't even showered."

"Molly!" Josie stamped her feet.

"I'm good to go," Grandpa Mac said. He was dressed in plaid pajama pants and the World's Best Grandpa T-shirt I bought for him this Father's Day. "And thank you for that basket, Josie. It's beyond my wildest dreams."

Josie looped her arm through Grandpa Mac's. "We're just so glad you came. Raine's sure missed you a lot." She pulled Grandpa Mac out through the door, and left the rest of us to follow. "Our sheds have been off-limits," she told Grandpa Mac. "So everything inside them is a secret. Raine's the only person who's seen my work in progress."

"Raine?" Mama frowned. "You went into Josie's shed?"

"Oh, forget about it, Molly," Josie interrupted. "It's too late for Raine to get in trouble. And I needed Raine's great wisdom to go forward with my art."

Inside Josie's shed, everything looked different. The scraps of cloth were gone. Every inch was clean. Still there was the smell of cinnamon and Christmas. On the table in the corner, Josie's pile of memory patches sat waiting to be stitched into a quilt. "Ta-da!" She pointed toward her artwork on the wall. "So?" She threw her arm over my shoulder. "Did I get the feelings right, Raine?"

We all stood there silent, staring. Josie's fabric scraps and shapes had turned into a story. A giant wall quilt covered with the haunted shapes of orphans, the rows of beds, the hills, and above the house their parents floated through the sky. A long black strip of ribbon split the quilt in half. There was Sparrow Road on one side, and on the other was the world.

For Lillian and Nettie and Lyman and the children. Josie's embroidered words were scattered like dust across the quilt.

"Wowee, woo-woo-woo," Diego whistled. "Josie girl, you're totally amazing. It takes my breath away."

"Mine too," I said. "*What was or what could be?*"

Diego caught my eye. "Yep," he said.

"But it's so sad," Mama sighed.

Grandpa Mac put his palm on Mama's back. "Very sad indeed."

Before we stepped into Diego's shed,
I reached up and blinded Mama's eyes. "Wait!" I said. "Before you see Diego's work, you have to promise me one thing."

Mama tugged my hands away. "What?" she asked like she didn't trust me.

"You have to show your art today. You have to sing at least one song at the party. One song with your guitar. And if you do, I'll read my story to the group." All week, Mama had been begging me to read my writing at the party. One story. Anything. And now that mine was finished, I was ready to trade it for her song.

"Raine's right," Diego said. "You have to sing. You'll sing and Raine will read. Art by the O'Rourkes. What more could anybody want?"

"No," Mama sighed.

"She does sing like an angel," Grandpa Mac said. "The best voice I've ever heard. Molly had a music scholarship to college."

"Dad," Mama groaned, embarrassed.

"So?" I grabbed on to Mama's hand. "Your song for my story?" Mama was an artist as much as everybody else. I didn't want Mama acting like a servant at the party, just pouring drinks and putting cookies out on platters. I wanted her to sing the way she did that day at the cathedral. The day Gray first fell in love.

"Okay, okay," Mama said. "I'll think about one song."

The second she said it everybody clapped.

"Enough!" Mama said. "Let's see Diego's work."

"This is it," Diego said when we stepped inside his shed. He pointed to an old door propped against one wall. It was plastered with a mishmash of odd items: buttons, shells, seeds, the plastic spoon from the ice cream social, the Orange Crush cap Josie snatched up off of the ground, labels off of pickle jars cut into tiny pieces and pasted into trees, a broken clothespin, dried wildflowers from the woods, a faded photo cutout of Mama planting in the garden, a pencil sketch of me writing underneath the willow. The sparrow feather I found in the field. Tiny scraps of Josie's velvet were glued along the edge. A line from Lillian's poem floated through the center like a wave. *There will never be a way to save one summer.* It was like a mosaic of our days made from a thousand tiny pieces of found junk. And it was beautiful and peaceful—golden and lavender and green—as if all these odds and ends were meant to come together in a picture. It reminded me of sunset or the way the morning sun sparkles white against the grass and then it's gone.

"So?" Diego winked at me. "My *what if or what could be?*"

"If someone opened up that door, they'd walk straight into our summer," I said. I wanted to stare at it forever.

"That was my hope," Diego said to me. "The door to Sparrow Road."

Grandpa Mac crossed his arms over his chest. "Who'd have guessed," he said, "that you could make something this pretty out of garbage?"

"Diego guessed," I said. "Diego guessed it all."

44

"I suppose I better put some of those cookies back into the freezer," Mama said.

We'd baked sweets to serve at least two hundred guests, but so far the Arts Extravaganza looked like it might get twenty people tops. The few who came took a cup of lemonade, grabbed one of Mama's cookies, but most seemed too out of place to speak. None of them stopped off at our stations to make art. All these weeks I'd pictured our Arts Extravaganza as a giant carnival with banners on the highway and Christmas lights twinkling in the trees. But now it felt more like the rummage sale at church. Hot and dull and sticky. Grandpa Mac's pail of penny candy melted in the sun.

"I'll help you with those, Molly." Grandpa Mac grabbed a second tray of cookies and followed Mama to the house. Josie stood out in the driveway greeting the two or three new visitors who came. I set up my doll stand. Lillian sat beside me with a stack of Josie's napkins for people to embroider. Gray still hadn't come.

"It's a flop," I said to Diego. Where were all the people who packed the Rhubarb Social? Why didn't they come to Sparrow Road? Dave from the Comfort Cone wasn't even there.

Diego sat down at my station. "It's early, Raine. And in the meantime, I'm ready to get started on a doll."

"First you need a question," I said.

"Got it." Diego winked. "I've had it for a while, Raine." Diego traced the pattern on a piece of flowered sheet. "You promise me an answer?"

"It worked for me." I looked out toward the driveway; I didn't understand why Gray was late. "Unless it's about a real date with Mama. Then you can just ask me. I'm pretty sure Mama would say yes."

Diego laughed. "Isn't there some rule about the question being secret? Like the wish you make before you blow out the candles on your birthday cake?"

"No rules," I said.

"Of course," he roared. "No rules! Josie made it up."

When Gray's old van finally pulled into the driveway, I was glad Grandpa Mac was in the house with Mama. "Your dad's here," Diego said.

My heart skipped. I didn't know what I'd say to Gray or how Grandpa Mac would treat him; I just wanted that hard part of the party to be done.

"Go on, I'll supervise your stand. I've got the dolls down now. And Raine?" He tugged on my shirt. "Your

Grandpa Mac and Gray? They just want to see you happy. Your mama, too. You're all on the same team." He gave my back a quick "go get 'em" pat. "They just don't know it yet."

You're all on the same team. Diego's words sounded strong and definite and happy. Just the way I wanted things to be.

Gray lugged an old guitar case, more scuffed and scabbed than the one he'd given Mama. "Hey there, Raine," he said, a toothpick stuck between his teeth.

"You ought to give that up," I said. "You're done with smoking." I didn't want him gnawing on a toothpick when he first met Grandpa Mac. Or met him again as the Gray who didn't drink.

"This?" Gray took the toothpick out and slipped it back into his shirt pocket. "I'll do my best." He looked around the almost empty driveway. "It's slow on the front end, I see."

"No one's coming," I said.

"They'll come. Comfort folks won't be here in a rush but they'll be here," he drawled. "Your grandpa make it in okay?" I could tell he held a little hope my answer might be no.

"He's here," I said. "He finally got here yesterday. And this morning we got to see Josie and Diego's art. I can't wait for you to see it. And Josie made him his own breakfast basket."

"A breakfast basket?" Gray asked.

I'd already forgotten Gray wasn't part of Sparrow Road in the beginning. "Oh, it's something Josie makes. With painted eggs and other things. She left one at our door the first morning we were here."

"That sure sounds sweet." I could tell that he felt bashful, like the guests who still didn't touch our cookies.

"Want a glass of lemonade?" I asked.

"Not yet." Gray leaned a little with his case.

"Grandpa Mac won't punch you," I said. "He promised me. And he's sorry that he ever did." I lied about that last part, but I didn't want Gray to wonder and worry through the party.

"I'm certain I deserved it." Gray rubbed his jaw. "But I don't want to bring trouble to your party." He reached back into his pocket for a toothpick and then he let it go.

"There won't be trouble," I said. "Grandpa Mac knows that you quit drinking. He knows all that is done."

"It's more a question of believing." Gray pushed the bangs back from his face.

"We're all on the same team," I said.

Gray's shoulders dropped a bit. "I don't imagine your grandpa would be too happy to hear that. Your mama either, for that matter. They don't much want me on their team."

"I do," I said. "I want you on my team."

Gray grinned his crooked grin. "I'm always on your team, Raine."

What happened next was the first shock of the party— Mama and Grandpa Mac both walked out to the driveway like Gray was some long-lost family they were truly glad to see. "Gray," Mama said. She was extra beautiful that day; her red curls fell long and soft over her shoulders, and she wore the long white sundress that made her look like an angel sent from heaven. Her feet were bare like the day Gray saw her sing, and she'd tied a row of Josie's braided bracelets on her wrists. "My dad," she said, as if Grandpa Mac and Gray had never met.

Grandpa Mac reached out and shook Gray's hand, the same friendly way he'd greeted all the artists.

"Sir," Gray said.

"Sir isn't really necessary." Grandpa Mac wrapped me in his arm. "Just Mac will do the trick." Grandpa Mac looked twice the size of Gray. "I hear you're going to play." He nodded at the guitar case in Gray's hand.

"If that's a thing Raine wants," Gray said. "I'm just here to follow orders." He smiled at me.

"Ah, Raine." Mama shook her head at me. "She's been wound up all day. I'm afraid she's turning into Josie. On Raine's orders we've got four hundred cookies in the freezer." It was the most I'd ever heard Mama say to Gray.

"Folks are on their way," Gray said. A few more cars had pulled into the driveway. "You wait and see. Raine will have her party."

"She sure will." Grandpa Mac hugged me closer. "She sure will have it, Gray."

It wasn't long before the front lawn was packed with people, and Gray sang his slow songs on the porch, and kids ran wild with long ropes of Grandpa Mac's red licorice, and most of Mama's cookies had been eaten and I had a long line of people waiting to make Eureka Dolls.

"What'd I tell you, Raine?" Josie shouted over all the noise. She was plopped down next to Lillian. Viktor had just come back from Comfort with more lemonade and cookies for the crowd. "Everybody came!"

"How's it going, honey?" Grandpa Mac dumped a fresh box of fabric scraps into my basket. Our Arts Extravaganza was bigger than I ever dreamed.

"You go ahead and work the crowd," Mama said to Josie. "I'll sit here with Lillian. I can paint faces from this station."

"You sure?" Josie stood and scanned the crowd. "I do have a couple of details to take care of."

"Go," Mama said to Josie, but it was my station I wanted her to work. I was tired of teaching people to make Eureka

Dolls; I wanted to grab my own fistful of candy, stop by Diego's station and create my own collage. I wanted to sit up on the porch and listen to Gray sing. In all the flurry, I'd missed most of his songs.

"Raine!" Josie glowed. "Look, look! Nettie Johnson came!" Josie pointed toward the driveway where Nettie Johnson and the reverend stood staring at the house.

"Nettie!" Josie hollered as she dashed across the lawn.

Viktor carried Lillian's Dream Chair to the front edge of the porch. "It looks like it's almost time to close your station," Mama said. "Viktor must be getting ready now to read." Just this morning, Viktor had agreed to read Lillian's poems. "And after that Eleanor." Mama wrinkled up her nose. "Then finally, it's your story! I can't wait to hear what you've been writing in that sketchbook. The crowd is going to love it, Raine."

My heart raced; suddenly the porch looked like a stage, a place where I didn't want to stand. Lyman's story was waiting in the attic, but now that there were so many faces at the party—so many kids my age scattered in small packs—I didn't want to read it to the crowd. "I don't know," I said. It felt safer to keep it tucked inside myself.

"Raine, Raine," Josie interrupted. She shoved a big brass bell into my hand. Her face was flushed, her eyes brighter than they'd ever been. "It's time to close the stations. We have to get the crowd to the front lawn. You go around the grounds and ring. Go gather people up."

"Everyone?" I said. People had strayed down to the lake.

"Yes!" Josie said, like I was Paul Revere. "Gather up the group. Make sure everybody comes."

I found people in the artists' sheds, people on the path down to the lake, people lingering in the parlor. There were people on the porch, people chatting in the shade. I told them all to head out toward the yard, but I didn't ring that crazy bell.

"Everybody," Josie shouted. She clapped her giant hands for quiet. There might have been two hundred people, maybe more, spread out on our front lawn. Dave from the Comfort Cone was there, and Leif, and Marge from the Blue Moon, and Dot, the Comfort Kitchen waitress who knew Gray's order by heart. "I want to thank you all for coming," Josie said. She looked like a wild rainbow standing in the center. "For joining us for Sparrow Road's First Annual Arts Extravaganza. For coming here to see the good work that's been done. And I want to give a special thanks to Viktor Berglund, a man who's made Sparrow Road a shelter through some storms. A place for peace and dreams."

Up on the porch, Viktor slouched into himself. He inched his chair closer to Lillian. Gray stretched out on the bottom step. In the front row, Diego had his arm over Mama's shoulder. Grandpa Mac stood alone under a tree. I wished someone was standing next to me.

"First," Josie said, "Viktor Berglund will read us poems by Lillian Hobbs. Then we'll have an essay by Eleanor

Dayton. And then we'll have a piece by our youngest, brightest artist—the amazing Raine O'Rourke." I wanted to crawl under the porch or run back to the cottage and hide under my bed. Josie swept her arm toward me while everybody clapped. I wasn't any kind of artist. I was a kid whose mother was the cook.

I was so sick with nerves and fear,
I hardly heard a word of Lillian's poetry. I only heard
the blood beating in my ears. When Viktor finished and
Eleanor stood up to read her essay, I ducked out of the
crowd and escaped up to the attic. I'd left Lyman's story
sitting on a bed.

"Hey," Gray called up the attic stairs. "I saw you sneak
away. Your act will be up soon."

"I don't want to read." The last time I'd been this scared
was when Sister Cyril made me read one of my stories to
the school in fourth grade. Until today, I'd forgotten how
much I hated standing on a stage. "Too many people here
today."

"It's the same for me before I sing," Gray said. "Stage
fright. Get it every time."

"You do?" I didn't think anyone who sang on a stage
could be afraid of people watching.

"Always had a problem with my nerves," Gray said. "It's
hard to put your heart out to a crowd. Not knowing what's

going to happen if you do. If folks will laugh or clap. Boo. It's hard to take that chance."

I pressed Lyman's story to my chest; I didn't want anyone to laugh at Lyman's words.

"But I just try to tell myself I've got the strength. And then I disappear inside the song."

"You disappear?"

"Yep. It's a trick I made up in my mind. You might be able to do it with your story. Just tell yourself you're going for a walk. Forget you're up on stage. Disappear while the words do all the work. Come on back when the audience starts clapping."

I couldn't imagine disappearing while I was reading to a crowd.

"Works for me," Gray said. "It might just work for you. Nerves run in our family." Our family. It made my heart fill just to hear Gray say it. He stared at Lyman's drawing. "Boy," he said, "that's lonely. Hills and hills of nothing. It sure is something else." Through the broken attic window we could hear the people clapping. "All that thunder for sour Eleanor. If the crowd liked her, you know you'll be a big-time hit." Gray gave a little laugh, and even his slow laughter sounded like a song. "Come on," he said. "Let's go take that walk."

At first Gray stood beside me on the porch, long enough for me to get my courage. Then I swallowed hard, opened up my mouth, and let Lyman tell his story.

What Was

   By Lyman Chase, Age 12

He spoke. And I went for a walk.

People think we didn't have parents. We had parents. Everybody does. I had parents, and I always knew that true fact in my heart. Even if I didn't have solid proof, a piece of paper or a picture, or someone to visit here on Christmas, or a dad to teach me to play baseball. I knew I had people out there somewhere. A father who held me in his heart. Thought about me. A mama too. People who liked to wonder what I might be doing. How I was growing up. Was I okay living in an orphanage? People who wondered hard about who I'd turn out to be. Same way someone wonders about a dog that ran away, or a friend they lost when they were little. All those missing things.

   And I always dreamed my parents wished that they could raise me. Maybe in a small place in the city, or a farm out in the country. One with a red barn and an old black horse I could ride across the hills.

   But that chance never came. Or else they would have taken me back home.

   I wish I knew exactly where they were, what they looked like, but no one ever told me. And not knowing was the hardest thing to bear. Lots of times I waited for a letter, everybody did, but letters never came. And sometimes I'd stand up in the attic and stare out at the hills, especially in winter when everything was white, wishing they'd

surprise me with a visit, would walk across those hills, leave their
heavy footprints in the snow. And then my dad would come up to the
attic, open up a suitcase, and tell me, "Pack your things, we're leaving.
We can't take the missing anymore."

Then they'd take me with them to whatever kind of life that they
were living. Rich or poor. Good or bad. We'd make it as a family.

I must have dreamed that dream a thousand times at least. Year
after year, looking out my window.

But they never came to get me.

And then those years were gone.

When the final line was finished I came back from my
walk; the place was pounding with applause. Gray was
right; I could let Lyman tell his story. His words did all
the work. Out in the crowd, I saw Grandpa Mac wipe a
tear off of his cheek. Then Mama too. Maybe tears ran
in the O'Rourke family. Josie howled above the din, and
Diego clapped his hands over his head. Gray looked up
and gave a quiet grin.

"Okay, okay," Josie said. "We have one more big event.
Don't leave yet." Josie stood behind Lillian's rocker, her
big hands clamped on Lillian's small shoulders. Viktor's
hands were pressed together, his forehead resting on his
fingers. He didn't even look up. "Our poet Lillian Hobbs
is our great joy." Josie's voice boomed above the crowd and
pretty soon the hum of conversation stopped. Bored kids

straggled to the backyard or disappeared inside the house. "Our daily treasure."

I sat down on the step with Gray. "You sure got a gift with words," Gray whispered. He twirled the toothpick in his fingers but he didn't stick it in his teeth.

"I don't know," I said. If I had a gift with words, Gray James had passed it on.

"Not so many years ago," Josie said, "Lillian taught at Sparrow Road. Back when it was an orphanage."

Lillian? Why was Josie talking about Lillian? It was time for Mama's song.

"I taught piano." Lillian blinked. "And I helped the children with their spelling."

"Yes," Josie said. "You did." She turned back to the crowd. "And Lillian gave her life and heart to lots of kids who lived without their parents. Many, many children. And for all of them, she tried to make Sparrow Road a home. A place where they felt safe. So today, some of those children have come to honor her, have come home to Sparrow Road."

Those children? Viktor lifted up his head and stared out at the crowd. Did Josie mean the orphans? Wasn't Nettie Johnson the only orphan that we knew?

"Me?" Lillian raised her hand up to her throat. Her voice wobbled. "Here to honor me?" She looked around the yard.

"You," Josie said. "For all the good you gave to Sparrow Road."

I looked across the yard. Nettie Johnson and the reverend stood off in a cluster of people near the pines. Were these the kids who lived at Sparrow Road? The orphans Josie and I imagined all this time? They didn't look sad like Josie's quilt. They didn't look anything like the way I pictured Lyman. They were ordinary people, no different from the folks who shopped at Grandpa Mac's.

"We're lucky," Josie continued, "when we get a chance to thank someone in their lifetime. It's why people came today from as far away as Florida." I heard a quick break in Josie's big strong voice.

"Tallahassee," a man yelled from the crowd.

"Florida?" Lillian looked confused.

"They came for you," Josie said. "So I'll just let them have their say."

She motioned for Nettie Johnson and her cluster to come up to Lillian's chair. The entire crowd sat silent; no one even coughed. The first person to speak was a man in a black suit. His thin white hair was slicked perfect to the side.

"Miss Hobbs," he said to Lillian. "I'm sure you don't remember me. John Schram. The kid who couldn't spell." He cleared his throat. "Well, I grew up to be a teacher. A principal. And I still can't spell too well." A wave of laughter moved over the lawn.

"You just need more practice," Lillian said. "Everyone can spell well if they try."

"That's what you always said." John Schram looked down at his paper; like me, he didn't want to see the crowd. "You always said I could do anything. And so I did."

"You were always a smart boy," Lillian said.

"And you said that to everybody," John Schram said. The whole crowd laughed again. "She did," he said to us. "She tried to make us all believe that we were brilliant."

"The children are all brilliant," Lillian said. "Just because we're waiting for our parents, it doesn't mean we don't have gifts."

"That's what you said to me." John Schram rolled the piece of paper in his hand. "And I remember once, when I was ten or twelve, a family came to look at me. They looked at me and then they took Clay Smith instead. I wanted out of Sparrow Road then in the worst way, and I remember crying in the attic and you came up and told me I was lucky. You said there were bigger things ahead for me than working someone's farm. You said I'd do great things someday. And Miss Hobbs, you made me believe it." John Schram choked on his last words. "Thank you," he said to Lillian.

He bent down and kissed her on the cheek. I could see the tears welling in his eyes.

There were eight or nine who stood up and told stories about Lillian—Lillian teaching them piano, Lillian with her pockets full of lemon drops, Lillian reciting poems to them before they went to sleep. One woman remembered how Lillian kept watch beside her bed while she was sick with scarlet fever, and another talked about the way Lillian taught fractions by dividing up a single bar of chocolate she bought for them herself. Several people said she always told them how much their parents missed them. How it did their hearts good to know that they were loved, even if their parents couldn't be with them.

"Our parents always love us," Lillian said. "Even when they leave. They hold us in their hearts."

"Every day," Gray whispered. I was so lost in their stories, I'd forgotten he was there.

The last man to get up didn't look much older than Gray. James Delgado had a full black beard and mass of thick black curls. "I was one of the last to leave," he said to the crowd. "I was in the final group they put in foster families just before Sparrow Road shut down." He looked up at the house. "And as tough as we all thought this place was, how much we hated living in an orphanage—" He stopped and wiped his hand across his forehead. "Our problems didn't disappear by closing Sparrow Road. I went through seven foster families before I turned eighteen. Some were kind, but some were truly terrible."

A hum of uneasiness drifted through the crowd. "I'm sure that's why I grew up to study foster care myself. I've come to Sparrow Road many times. I've sat here in this driveway and I've walked over these fields. And I've tried to decide what should be done with kids whose parents just can't keep them. For all the reasons parents have to give their children up. And after all these years, I still don't have an answer. It isn't Sparrow Road; I know that. But it also isn't going house to house, hoping one good family sticks."

"Miss Hobbs," he said to Lillian. "I think you did the only thing that can be done. You loved all the ones that no one else did." He scratched his bushy beard. "We have to love the children that are left. Because someone has to do it. And I knew that you loved me."

"I did," Lillian said. "I loved you all. But I'm sure it's time the children had their supper. I don't like to leave them hungry for too long."

She stood up from her chair and swayed. A gasp rose from the lawn. Viktor lunged forward and held her steady on her feet. I'd never seen Viktor move so fast.

"I'm fine," she said. "The children love the cookies."

"Maybe a rest," Viktor said. "This day has been too much."

"A lovely party," Lillian nodded. "But I'm ready for a nap."

48

"Raine," Nettie Johnson called. She was standing by herself near the path to the infirmary. After all the speeches, the front lawn crowd had thinned. People gathered at the stations, others crossed the field to see the artists' sheds. "Could I speak to you a minute?"

When I got over to the tree, Nettie Johnson was pulling a wad of tissue from her purse. "This is quite a day for me, hearing all those stories. Going back into this house." A bright white boat sailed across her sweatshirt. "I'm glad I came today. Very glad. It helps to be with other orphans. People who know what it was like." Nettie dabbed beneath her nose. "That story that you wrote. Did you really just imagine it?"

I nodded.

"But how?" she said. I wasn't going to tell Nettie Johnson how much I dreamed of Lyman, or how he was so real to me I saw him clearly in my mind. "How did you know what it felt like to be an orphan? Are you an orphan, dear?"

"No," I said.

"Then how?" She stared at me. "Because it really was exactly like you said."

"I don't know." I shrugged. "I just wrote how it felt to miss a parent. To want them back. To never know. To always have to wonder."

"Yes." Nettie took a powder compact from her purse and puffed a fluff underneath each eye. "All of that was in there. It's a subject you must know."

I walked with Nettie Johnson to the attic, where the orphans who'd returned were telling tales of Sparrow Road. The men told how cold the attic was in winter, so cold they could sometimes see their breath, and in the summer the heat made it impossible to sleep. James Delgado remembered the sound of constant winter coughs from asthma and pneumonia; John Schram remembered kneeling on the splintered floor at night to pray.

"The girls slept on the second floor," Nettie Johnson said to me. "We weren't allowed up in this attic."

When we finished with the attic, we all walked to the turret room that led up to the tower. "They kept that trapdoor sealed with metal and barbed wire," one woman said. "From the outside, that tower made the house look like a fairy tale, but no prince ever came to save me."

"Me either." Nettie Johnson touched the reverend's shoulder. "Although I found my prince eventually."

In every room the orphans had a memory—polishing

the woodwork, the nursery rhymes Lillian recited in the room where the little girls slept, the yellow wallpaper with Bo Peep and her sheep, the way they ate dinner at eight tables crammed into one room, the front parlor where they weren't allowed to sit, the library where they weren't allowed to read, the curving staircase they never got to take, the side parlor with the fireplace where kids met prospective parents.

"So few of us were taken," the woman who had had scarlet fever said. "And those that were weren't always treated well. I'm glad it wasn't me."

"I liked my family in Spring Valley," Nettie Johnson said. "But I'm sorry for you, James. All those foster families."

James Delgado shrugged. "What can you do?"

Listening to their stories, I knew Josie's broken quilt had been exactly right. Even after all this time, it still hurt them to remember.

"I'd like to organize a full reunion," Josie said. She picked up a tin of Mama's oatmeal cookies and passed it through the room. A full reunion? Hadn't our Arts Extravaganza been enough? "Maybe have a weekend where we open up the house to all the kids who lived at Sparrow Road. Paint a mural in their memory. Do a sculpture garden. Some work of art to commemorate their lives. And we can write down all their stories." I stared at Josie, stunned. Did she just hatch this scheme in the middle of our party?

"I don't know," Nettie Johnson said. "Our stories might be better left untold."

"Oh no," Josie said. "We need to know your stories. People need to know how it feels to be a child without parents and what we can do to help, so we can carry on the good work Lillian did. Letting all the children know they're loved. Giving homes to kids who go without. The people here today, some of them passed you on the street when you were kids in Comfort. And they just thought you were odd. Orphans. A thing out of the ordinary they wanted to avoid. They didn't have a clue what it felt like to be you. Until today."

"No," John Schram said. He took a bite of Mama's cookie. "They definitely didn't."

49

By the time we'd finished up our tour, and the orphans had glued their cards and letters and memories and drawings into a scrapbook that said *Miss Hobbs* on the front, and I'd finally had a glass of lemonade and made a quick collage at Diego's messy station, and Mama had her feet up on a milk crate, and Grandpa Mac was sleeping on a hammock in the shade, and Gray and Viktor collected litter off the lawn, the Comfort folks had dwindled to a few.

"Same time next year!" Josie bounced up on the toes of her black boots.

Next year we wouldn't live here, none of us but Viktor. New artists would arrive to take our place. Someone else would work in Josie's shed. Maybe another cook would live in our small cottage. *"What if or what could be?"* I said, which was easier than thinking Sparrow Road was ending for us all.

"Exactly." Josie grinned. "You think Lillian was happy?"

"Yes," I said. "I think she really was."

"Molly," Diego called. He held out Mama's black guitar case. "You still owe Raine her song."

"Oh no!" I moaned. "Mama, you didn't play!" In all the blur of the party—the stations, the crowds, the stories of the orphans, Nettie Johnson—I'd forgotten Mama's promise for a song. And now the crowd wasn't even here to hear it.

"Another time." Mama smiled, relieved. "I'll play another day."

"Play now!" I begged. "I'm sorry I forgot." I didn't want Mama to be the only one without an art to show.

Grandpa Mac climbed out of the hammock. "Play it for us, Molly. You've got more talent than most people ever dream of."

"That sure would be my memory," Gray said. He set a bag of garbage on the grass.

Diego opened up the case and handed Mama the guitar.

"Come on," I said. "You promised. My story for your song."

For a long time, she just fiddled with the thing, turning knobs and plucking at the strings like she was trying to find the perfect sound. "I don't know what to sing." Mama's mop of red curls spilled over her guitar. She looked just like the young girl from our pictures.

"Give a try with 'Lucky.'" Gray had told me that was the song that Mama sang the first day he saw her on the street.

"Please," I said. "Please sing it for me, Mama."

"Oh, Raine." Mama heaved a heavy breath. "I can't play that song." She looked at Gray.

"I would doubt that, Molly," Gray said. "You sure could play it once."

"Play anything," Diego urged. He was standing close to Mama, close enough to be sure she didn't put that guitar back in its case.

"It all sounds good coming from you, Molly," Grandpa Mac said.

"Okay, okay." Mama plucked a few more notes and then her voice drifted over our front lawn and everybody's heart stopped. Mama's voice bubbled like a brook. Clear and clean. *"Life is fast, but love lasts long,"* Mama sang. She sent her sweet song straight to me; she didn't go out walking—she was inside every word. *"Take my heart and save my song—."*

Mama stumbled like she couldn't remember what notes she should play next. Then her clear voice broke a little bit. *"You and I are lucky to be here."*

Mama stopped. She pressed her hands against the strings to make them quiet and then she glanced at Gray. I saw something secret pass between them, something connected to the song, something that had happened before me. Maybe back when the two of them really were in love. I wanted Mama to keep going.

"That's it?" I said. "That was the whole song?"

"That's the whole song for today," Mama said. She shook her head and put the old guitar back in its case. "Show's over." She looked at Gray again.

Then Gray clapped slowly, so I started to clap too. "Molly," he said. "You could break a hundred hearts with that one song."

It was late that night before Grandpa Mac and I finally made it to the lake; so late the last sliver of orange sun was sinking low behind the hills. Two oil lanterns flickered on the shore. "Wait until the sun is gone, you won't believe the stars." I held the old boat steady while Grandpa Mac tumbled to his seat.

"I'll tell you what I can't believe, Raine," Grandpa Mac said. "I can't believe how grown up you've gotten. That here you are rowing a boat all by yourself. And the story about that boy you read today. I don't know how you dreamt up such a thing. Or how you threw that first-class party, but you did." Grandpa Mac laughed. "Good thing I got to see it for myself."

"I'll tell you what I can't believe," I said back to Grandpa Mac. "How nice you were to Gray today. I was so glad you didn't punch him in the face."

"I did my best," Grandpa Mac said. "I didn't want to spoil your party." He propped his elbows on his knees. "I like him better sober, that's for sure."

I was glad I didn't remember the Gray James who was drunk. To me, he'd always be the gentle soul who rescued Mr. Bones, the man who gave me his medallion, the kind singer who taught me how to disappear. I rowed us out into the middle of the lake; then I set the oars down against the side, let the muscles in my arms rest a little bit.

"You want me to take my turn?" Grandpa Mac asked. "It's getting mighty dark out here."

"Nope," I said. "I can do it by myself."

"I'm sure you can." Grandpa Mac leaned forward, his yellow life vest squished into his jaw. "But Raine, even all grown up, you still can't be too certain about Gray. Drinkers stop, but some of them go back. And drinkers—"

"Grandpa Mac," I said. "Gray isn't Mr. Earle."

"No," Grandpa Mac agreed. "But I'd hate to see you hurt."

Grandpa Mac had the same worried warning voice he always had at home. I didn't want to go back to all that worry. So much worry that he and Mama hardly let me leave the house alone. "It's okay," I said. "Even if Gray drinks again—" I stopped; I wasn't really sure how to end that sentence. If Gray drank again, then what? If he drank again, I guess I'd lose him twice. "If that happens, I think I'll be okay." I had enough strength in me to make it through the world whether Gray James drank again or not. Hope. I rolled the silver charm against my thumb.

"I suppose you're right about that, Raine. You're always

right." Grandpa Mac cleared his throat like he was fighting back a cough. "And whatever happens next, we'll always stay a family."

"Next?" I said. Grandpa's *next* sounded like a mystery. "What do you mean, what happens next? We'll be home in just a couple of weeks."

"Let's hope," he said. "Your mama sure does like it here. And you were right about these stars, Raine. I've never, ever seen so many in my life."

Across the still, black water, a blizzard of white stars glistened through the darkness. "Grandpa Mac," I said. "I'm so happy that you came."

"Me too. I wouldn't have missed this chapter for the world."

51

Grandpa Mac left me that next morning.
Left me standing in the driveway with the sad sense that
Sparrow Road was finally winding down. My summer dis-
appearing.

"Well, it's starting," Mama sighed when Grandpa Mac
was gone. "Diego leaves next week. They need him at his
college. His teaching begins before September."

"I can't believe it's going to end," I said. My heart
was already hanging heavy from telling Grandpa Mac
good-bye.

"Things do." Mama took my hand and we headed
toward the main house. Mama said she wanted to make
Lillian some breakfast; day by day Lillian seemed to
shrink a little smaller, seemed to make less sense.

Inside the shadowy front room, Eleanor sat silent on
the sofa, two bulging suitcases waiting at the door.

"You're leaving?" I asked. I wasn't disappointed, just
surprised. I couldn't wait for her to go.

"Yes." Eleanor smoothed her perfect skirt. "Despite a summer of distractions, my book is finally done. And after yesterday—all that horrible talk of orphans, children missing parents—well, I have to say, it made me eager to get home."

"I'm sure your daughters will be happy," Mama said politely. I didn't think anyone would be happy to see Eleanor, but then I thought of Lyman's story—*Rich or poor. Good or bad.* Horrible as she was, Eleanor's children probably loved her.

"Yes," Eleanor said stiffly. "And despite what you might think, it was difficult for me to have a child here while mine were far away. Very difficult."

"I understand." Mama hugged me close. The two of us did better when we faced Eleanor together. "I couldn't spend a summer without Raine."

"Well, you had your time together," Eleanor said. She turned to me. "And Raine, that story that you read? The one about the orphan? I saw some early promise in that work. Perhaps, like me, you'll grow up to be a writer."

If I grew up to be a writer, I wouldn't be anything like her. I'd be a writer like sweet Lillian, someone kind to children. Or a writer who could find things in the clouds. Or believed in things that no one else could see.

"Here." She handed me a dictionary, so heavy I had to hold it with both hands. "It's an old one I brought with me from Boston. If you really hope to write, you need to work on your vocabulary. Learn to spell correctly. I wouldn't rely on Lillian for lessons."

"I know how to spell," I said. Lillian had taught me lots of things—like poetry and patience. And love. Things that mattered more than spelling.

"I'd recommend a page a day," Eleanor advised.

"A page a day?" I rolled my eyes. Mama pinched me hard; she still expected manners. "Well, thanks," I said.

"A decent dictionary," Eleanor said. "It's the most important thing a writer needs."

"Not dreams?" I asked. Diego never would have said to start a story with a dictionary. It took more than a dictionary to dream Lyman to life.

"Dreams?" Eleanor squinted like she couldn't quite understand me. "I don't know," she said. "I suppose a dream couldn't hurt."

Maybe it was Eleanor's departure, or the end of the Arts Extravaganza, but suddenly everything seemed different in the house. Summer wasn't summer anymore. Evenings, Josie sat with Lillian and sewed. Diego spent more time at our cottage, like he wished the days with Mama wouldn't end.

Mama finally said yes to a date. A drive-in movie stuck out in a field with gnats and mosquitoes swarming through the windows, and the actor's voices scratching through a rusted speaker. Josie and I supervised it all from the back end of Viktor's truck, our dirty feet up against the window, a bucket of buttered popcorn propped between us.

On their second date, they biked to the Comfort Cone alone.

After their third date, Mama came home and climbed into my bed. There was something important she had to tell me. Something that couldn't wait. I was sure she was going tell me news about Diego, but instead she told me Viktor had asked us both to stay.

"Stay?" I said. "You mean live at Sparrow Road?" I sat up in bed and pulled the sheet up to my chin. I wasn't cold, but still a shiver prickled down my spine. Was this the *next* that Grandpa Mac mentioned in the boat? "What about Milwaukee? I promised Grandpa Mac that we'd be back. And school? I'm starting seventh grade."

"I know," Mama whispered. "But you could go to school with the other kids in Comfort. And I'd watch over Lillian. Lillian isn't going to go back to St. Paul. She's aging, Raine. She's going to need more help. And I wouldn't have to be a waitress anymore."

I didn't want Mama to stay a waitress, or Lillian to be alone, or to live so far from Gray, but Grandpa Mac was waiting for his family. "No," I said. "We're going home. I gave Grandpa Mac my word."

"But Grandpa Mac would visit," Mama said. "I need to move on with my life, Raine. I can't live with Grandpa

Mac forever. Just like you'll grow up and move away from me."

"I won't." I nuzzled my nose into Mama's neck. It was enough to imagine giving up Milwaukee; I didn't want to dream about the day I wouldn't live with Mama anymore. I swallowed hard. All that orphan sadness was a part of me. Like Gray and Lillian, I was a soul who couldn't bear the getting left or leaving. "Have you made up your mind already?"

"No," Mama said. "Not without you, Raine."

52

What would you do if you were me?
I wrote to Lyman. Real or not, he always helped me think
my troubles through. I wondered if he'd go back with me
to Milwaukee, if I'd still be able to imagine him that far
from Sparrow Road. *If you had a grandpa waiting? Or made a
promise you knew you had to keep?*

I left my sketchbook on my lap desk, stood up in the
tower, and looked over the land. In Milwaukee, I'd only
have our bedroom for my dreams. And even then, half of
it was Mama's. And there'd be the constant noise of the
TV, or radio and telephones, cars honking on the street.
All the perfect silence would be gone. The night song of
the insects. The way the wind whistled through the weeds.

I didn't have a grandpa, Lyman finally said. *Or anybody
waiting.* He leaned on the ledge beside me. *But if I did, I guess
I'd keep my word.*

Even if it meant leaving things you loved?

There's lots of ways of leaving, Lyman said. *Even staying in one
place. You can't get through life without it.*

Below us, Viktor stood staring at his turtles, his hands deep in his pockets, his eyes set on the water. *People liked your story*, I said. *Especially the orphans.*

Even him? Lyman asked.

I don't know. Viktor never told me.

No? Lyman said. *He wouldn't.*

Lyman? Your friend that moved away? The one who left the marble underneath your pillow? Was it Viktor? Did he live here as an orphan? Did he leave here with the Berglunds? Did they take him to New York?

When I'd shown the lucky penny note to Lillian, she'd only said the writer was a boy with a big heart. No name she could remember. But the way she pressed the penny to her cheek told me that she knew.

Ask him, Lyman said. *Ask about the marble. Maybe your answer will be there.*

When Sunday morning came, I went down to Diego's shed to say so long. I knew we'd all be waving from the porch, but there were words I'd been carrying all week, things I had to say to him in private. The door was open. He stood at the center table packing boxes, dressed in the same Hawaiian shirt he wore that morning we first met. Of all the things I'd miss, I thought I'd miss Diego's bright joy most of all. I'd never met a man who had the gladness of Diego.

"Well! Welcome, Raine," he said, his smile bright and wide. "You must have read my mind. I've got something for you here." He reached into a box and pulled out a small collage. It was a cut-out photo of me and Gray together at the barbecue, our heads close in conversation, and all around us in bits and pieces of ripped paper the summer sky shimmered in the sun.

It was a thing I knew I'd save forever. A thing I'd love years and years from now.

"Thanks," I said. "So much." I owed so many thank-yous to Diego I didn't know where to start. "Did you get the answer to your question?" I asked instead. His Eureka Doll was sitting on the table. He hadn't finished sewing up her head.

"I got it on my end." He winked. "I'm waiting for your mama's answer now."

"I'll have her start her doll today." I smiled. I had a good idea what Diego might have asked, but I didn't want him to tell me. I already had too many what-ifs pressing on my brain.

Diego leaned against the table. "Boy oh boy. I wish I could stay."

"Me too," I said. "I mean, I wish the same for you." Through Diego's window I saw Josie and Lillian sewing in the sun. "You know, Viktor offered a home to me and Mama. He said that we could stay; Mama could have a job taking care of Lillian."

"Your mama told me," Diego said.

"But I'd miss Grandpa Mac." I slid my hope charm along its chain.

"On the bright side," Diego said, "you'd have more time with Gray. Time the two of you could use."

Gray was one of the many thank-yous I still had to tell Diego. I knew it was Diego who helped Mama find the strength to let me go to Gray. And it was Diego who first said Gray was my dad. *My dad.*

And it was Diego who taught me how to listen to my dreams, to settle into silence, to trust *what was or what could be.* It was Diego who left the lap desk up in the tower for me. Diego who said we were all on the same team.

"I don't know what to choose," I said. "Either way I lose."

"Or either way you win. But you never know the end at the beginning." His happy laughter boomed inside the shed. It was a sound I knew I'd miss a long, long time.

Those last lazy days of August, Gray and I were free to wander on our own. Gray taught me how to fish for sunnies, and I taught him how to bake a pineapple upside-down cake. Together, we climbed the highest hill from Lyman's drawing, and when we made it to the top we sat silent and stared at Sparrow Road. "It still looks sad to me," Gray finally said. "But maybe it's all the work I've got ahead. I'll be painting the outside of that place until November. November and then some." He gave me a little grin.

Mama let us drive all over Comfort taking pictures with a camera Gray bought me at the Comfort five-and-dime. One day we had a picnic at Good Shepherd with Mr. Bones tied on a leash. I told Gray stories of days he missed when I was little, and he showed me faded photos of his parents, Maw and Paw, his brother Bug, his sisters Peg and Little Lou. "These folks are all your family," he said. "You got lots of cousins, too. They'd all like to meet you someday, Raine."

Maybe by next summer Mama would let me travel to Missouri. By thirteen I'd be old enough to see my family for myself.

It felt like I was living wait and see, like I was torn between two choices. Go back to Milwaukee or stay at Sparrow Road. And it was up to me to say. Then one day Viktor drove us miles into the country to see the Comfort school, plunked down like the drive-in in a field.

"I'll wait here in the truck," Viktor said. "The two of you should see it for yourselves."

Mama and I walked the circle of the building. The grass was dry, the parking lot sat empty. Weeds grew wild in the field. "Well," Mama joked. "At least you would be safe here, Raine."

I tried to see myself starting over at a school with the kids I saw in Comfort. Country kids. It was one thing to live at Sparrow Road, to fish with Gray at Sorrow Lake, to help Josie plan the Second Annual Arts Extravaganza, to sit up in the attic and imagine Lyman's story, to read Lillian her poetry and practice stupid little kid songs on the piano—things other kids would never see. It was another to be the new girl sitting lonely during lunch. The weird kid who lived out with the artists. The girl without a single friend beside her on the bus.

"I can't stay," I finally choked. "Lillian and Gray. All of it. I have to say good-bye."

It was during one of Mama's nightly phone calls to Diego that Viktor found me on the bench beneath the willow.

"May I have a seat?" He parted the long curtain of thick leaves and sat down on the far end of the bench. In all my time here, Viktor had never asked to sit beside me; most days we still passed without hello.

"About my offer," Viktor said. "I had intended it to help. But sometimes help can be a kind of harm." He glanced up at the house. "Sparrow Road," he said. "When the Berglunds gave it to that charity, they hoped that it would help. But in the end—" He looked down at his hands. "No orphanage is happy. No matter what we hope."

"No," I said. "But at least they had a home. And they had Lillian to love them."

"Yes, Lillian," Viktor said. "Sometimes shelter is the best that we can offer." He pressed his fingertips together. Cleared his throat. "I hope there was some happiness this summer for you here."

"There was," I said, more happiness than I ever could explain. So much happiness my heart hurt. "And thanks for helping Gray," I said. "I know you let him live here after New Connections, and drove him to Milwaukee, and talked Mama into giving him a chance with me."

"I did very little." Viktor held his hand up as if I'd said enough. "Only what I could."

"Well, thanks," I said again.

"That story that you read?" Viktor rubbed his sunken cheek. "Lyman's? I believe he would have liked it very much."

"Lyman?" My heart leapt in my chest. "You knew Lyman?"

He stood, then slipped his hand into his pocket. "Yes," he said. "Once, I knew him very well." He drew back the leafy curtain. "I think it's what he would have wanted you to say." Then he took the first few steps of his nightly solitary stroll. Often, before I fell asleep, I'd see him in the meadow alone beneath the moon.

"Viktor?" I managed to squeak out. I still had one last mystery to solve. "Did you ever know a boy who left a marble under Lyman's pillow? Who taped a penny on a paper for Lillian?"

He stopped and stared at me. "Yes," he finally said. "I believe perhaps I did."

A shiver spread over my skin. "Were you an orphan once?"

"Was I?" He glanced up toward the attic. The lights were off. Bats hung under the eaves. There was nothing there to see, but still he looked. Then something in his face made me think of James Delgado. Nettie Johnson and John Schram. All the orphans at the Arts Extravaganza. Even Lillian and Lyman. It was the lost look of someone who'd been left. I already had the answer in my heart.

"I can hear it in your music."

"My music?"

"Yes," I said.

Then he turned back toward the meadow, his body a lanky silhouette against the setting sun. "Good night to you, Raine," he sighed. "You're really quite a girl."

I found Lillian and Josie on the front porch eating the last of Mama's cherry pie. A sea of votive candles flickered in glass jars. The song of shell chimes tinkled in the breeze. "My summer orphan," Lillian sighed.

"Grab a piece of pie, Raine." Josie straightened the shawl on Lillian's shoulders. It was watery blue velvet, the blue of Lillian's eyes, with beads and fringe and buttons and whatever other doodads Josie had sewn on this summer.

"Smells almost like September," I said. An August cool had already set in, and I could smell red leaves, and after that, the winter. I thought of Lyman, cold up in that attic, and the way the hills would look coated in pure white.

I sat down on the porch swing next to Lillian and thought of my first day. The lemon drop she gave me, the Old Maid cards she pulled out of her pocket, the way she made my homesick end.

"You got your stuff all packed?" Josie asked. She wasn't in any hurry to move out of Sparrow Road.

"Most," I said. I took a bite of Mama's cherry pie, sugary and sour. So tart it tingled on my tongue. "My writing desk is too big for the train." Diego said I should leave it as a gift to other writers, for another dreamer who liked to sit up in the tower. *Pass it on,* he'd said, *the way the Berglunds did.*

"Good reason for him to visit Milwaukee," Josie said. "He'll have to build a new one for you there."

"I guess." I tried to smile. A Milwaukee writing desk would never be the same.

"Is her father here?" Lillian put her fork down on her plate. "Is it time for her to leave?"

"He is." Josie patted at her hand. "But Raine won't be gone long."

"I left," Lillian said, "but not for long." She blinked at me. "You can come back to me if you're alone."

"I'm alone." Josie clapped her hands together. "And I'd live here forever if I could." She tugged on my wrist. "I think for old times' sake we'd better make one more nightly sojourn to that attic. By candlelight tonight. Give those missing kids one last good-bye."

Sitting silent in the attic, the yellow glow of candles casting shadows on the walls, I was sure I heard the heavy breath of James Delgado's asthma, John Schram finishing his prayers. And underneath it all, Viktor's symphony of sorrow. The sad cry of the violin, the moan of his piano.

Josie stretched out on a mattress, her big black boots pressed against the ceiling, the creak of metal springs sagging low beneath her weight.

I walked over to the wall and stared at Lyman's drawing; I wanted to remember it years and years from now.

I asked about the marble, I said inside myself. *He knew the boy who left it underneath your pillow.*

So you've solved your final mystery? Lyman smiled. *I guess you're ready now to leave?*

No, I said. *Not ready.*

"You memorizing, Raine?" Josie whispered in the darkness. "Gathering all the memories you want to take back to Milwaukee? That lonesome drawing? All the stories up here in the dust?"

"I can't memorize it all," I said. "There's too much for me to take."

I looked long at Lyman's snowy hills, ran my fingertip along the chalky waves. *I visited your hills,* I said. *I walked on them with Gray.*

You did? Lyman smiled, surprised. *I'd like to do the same someday. Walk them with my family.*

You will, I said. *When your father finally comes.*

55

Gray said that after all these years of waiting for hello he couldn't bear a sad "so long," so we had to settle on a "see ya soon" instead. Before the morning moon had faded from the sky, Gray knocked at our cottage. Then the two of us took our last slow stroll across the field until we stopped in the same place where we talked on that first night. But this time we stood there in a quiet that felt right for Gray and me. The two of us didn't always need to talk.

Behind us, the main house was lit up with our leaving and I could hear Mama talking to Viktor in the distance. "Your mama said I can visit in Milwaukee." Gray's bangs hung over his eyes. "I'll make the drive as soon as you want company. The minute that you say."

Truth was, I wanted Gray's company already. I couldn't imagine how lonely I'd feel those long hours on the train.

"Milwaukee's pretty far away," I said. I wasn't sure Gray would really make that drive—even if he said so.

"Not so far now." Gray grinned. "And I'll be going back to music soon. I got another record in me. I think I'll call it *Raine*."

"Raine with an *e*?"

"Yep," he said. "I don't think there's any other kind."

I shoved my cold hands into the front pouch of my sweatshirt. In the heat of summer, I hadn't worn it at all. It still smelled like our apartment in Milwaukee—Beauty's sleek black fur, Mama's morning coffee, the dryer in the basement. It was strange the way a place's smell held on. I hoped my summer clothes would hold on to Sparrow Road so I could slip into a shirt and be back here again.

Gray stared down at his cowboy boots. "Raine," he said, "the second chance you gave me—" He took a long, slow breath. He was struggling the same way I had struggled to say thank you to Diego. "You didn't need to do it, and I know it."

The morning moon was just beginning to fade quiet from the sky, and across the lake a silver fog hung over Lyman's fields. I thought about the thousand orphans and their leaving.

"It isn't just a chance," I said. I didn't want Gray to think there'd be another chance if he went back to drinking.

"No," he said. "I know it. It isn't just a chance, it's the way it's going to be now for our lives."

When we got back to the house, Josie, Lillian, and Mama had gathered in the driveway. Viktor waited in his truck.

"Molly." Gray gave his country shrug to Mama. A film of tears clouded his black eyes.

Mama put her arm around me. "It's what Raine wanted, Gray." I didn't know if she meant leaving Sparrow Road and going home to Grandpa Mac, or meeting Gray this summer, or taking him to be my father after all.

"Still," Gray said. I could see the fear and love he felt for Mama. "I thank you for it, Molly."

"It was Raine I did it for, Gray." Mama pressed her lips against my hair. "But you were right." Mama stumbled on that last word but still she said it. "Raine was old enough to know—" She left off in the middle. I waited for her to say *her father*, or *the truth*, but instead she just said, "You."

"My dad," I said.

"Yep," Gray said. "Your dad."

"And I'm glad I got to know everybody," Josie shouted. She stepped forward and squished me in a giant Josie hug. "And Raine just tops that list. Sparrow Road will miss you both," Josie said. "But I want you back here for our reunion in December. And this time, you bring Grandpa Mac along."

I glanced at Viktor. "A reunion in December? Did Viktor say it was okay?"

"Fear not!" Josie propped her big hands on her hips. "Let me worry about Viktor."

"Josie's staying," Mama said to me. "She took the offer Viktor made to us. She'll be Lillian's company."

"You're staying?" I couldn't believe wild Josie would live at Sparrow Road with Viktor. "But what about your job?"

"I'm happy where I'm needed, and it's Lillian who really needs me now. We're starting on piano right away! I want to get to 'Happy Birthday.'" Lillian and I never got that far. "And I know Diego won't miss our first reunion. Not with you and your mama here!" She gave a wink to Mama. "So, O'Rourkes, put it on your calendar. December."

"I'll be in Milwaukee before December." Gray rubbed his eye. "Heck, I might be there next week."

I tried to picture Gray in our apartment—Mama and Grandpa Mac in front of the TV while Gray and I talked at the kitchen table.

"And I've got to get to work on our Second Annual Arts Extravaganza," Josie said. "I'm already in touch with James Delgado. We're going to invite every orphan that we can. Hundreds. Can you imagine, Raine? So when you come back in December, we'll get started on our plans."

"Every orphan?" I glanced at Viktor waiting in the truck.

"I'm sure going to try." Josie gave me one last giant squeeze.

"Write me in Milwaukee," I said. "And I'll send letters back."

"Molly," Viktor called. "The train."

"I'll be back," I said to Lillian. I kissed her on the cheek the same way Diego always did. Her skin was old-cloth soft, like a nightgown that had finally worn thin. Or the baby blanket I rubbed down to a rag.

"Maybe not." Lillian pressed a penny into my palm. "Good luck, my summer orphan. You have a family now." Lillian patted at my shoulder.

"She does." Gray took a couple of timid steps in my direction. Then he opened up his arms like he was hoping for a hug.

I stepped forward just as timidly. I pressed my ear against his chest and listened to the beat of his shy heart. It was the first time in my life I'd hugged my dad.

"Milwaukee then," he whispered, but neither of us moved.

"Raine," Mama finally said. "We've got a train to catch this morning." She grabbed my hand and urged me toward the truck. I turned and gave a final wave; the same kind of half wave Gray gave that first day I saw him on the street. Then I didn't look back until I got into Viktor's truck.

Josie and Lillian stood waving from the porch. Gray stood where I'd left him in the driveway.

"See ya," Gray drawled again, and I was glad he didn't say it like a question.

"See ya," I called back.

Viktor turned the key. "Well, then," he said, and started down the driveway.

"December!" Josie yelled. "Don't forget our party!"

"Ah, Josie." Viktor shook his head. "I suspect she'll keep me busy."

Mama and I laughed. "Busier than you think," I said. Viktor would never keep up with Josie's schemes.

I turned and knelt up on the seat. Through the dusty rearview window I watched Lillian and Josie and Gray and the main house and the tower disappear behind the trees. Gone. *What was or what could be?* All that getting left and leaving. My stomach felt the way it had the first day I heard Gray's songs.

Diego said if I was really lonely, I could always write our story. Save our time here on the page, the way he had when he'd made his magic door to Sparrow Road. *And when you do*—he'd joked that last morning in his shed—*I want to be the handsome hero. The good guy who rides in on a white horse.* Even gone, I could still hear his giant, happy laugh.

Out on the highway I pulled my sketchbook from my backpack. Maybe I'd start on it today. My own memory quilt of stories. I could write it on the train before I got back to Milwaukee. Before I lost the smell of Sparrow Road. Before I was an ordinary girl again, holding a secret summer in her heart.

I tilted my sketchbook away from Mama's watchful eyes. I needed time to tell the story to myself.

Sparrow Road, I wrote.

It was a place for wishing long and dreaming, Lyman said to me.

Yes, I said. *It was.*

Acknowledgments

My gratitude to all who gave gifts to *Sparrow Road*: Mikaela, Dylan and Tim Frederick; Martin Case (infinite gifts, always), Robert Hedin, the Anderson Center, the Bush Foundation, Callie Cardamon, Elizabeth and Greg Brazil, Marilyn McNeal, Olivia Rowe, the Sisters of Clare's Well, Dick Stemper, Alana and Isabella Pixler, Deb Berendts, Molly Kenney, Mary Rockcastle, Chrissie Mahaffy, and the many artists whose great spirits inhabit *Sparrow Road*. Thank you to Rosemary Stimola for believing, and to the amazing Stacey Barney for delivering it with such love to the world.

Turn the page for a sample of
Sheila O'Connor's next book

KEEPING SAFE *the* STARS

1

WAIT

It was Old Finn who sent us down the wood path to Miss Addie's. First he kissed us each good-bye and told us not to worry, then he said to stay put in Miss Addie's tiny trailer until he came home from St. John's.

Which is exactly what we did—me and Nightingale and Baby—we sat there at Miss Addie's cutting photographs from movie magazines, building paper towns, and stringing necklaces from noodles. We waited and we worried, even though Old Finn had told us that we shouldn't.

When darkness finally came, I opened Miss Addie's tattered phone book and hunted down the number for St. John's Hospital in town. Old Finn didn't keep a phone up at our cabin. "It's been too long," I said. "Old Finn only went in for a fever."

"He must be sick," Miss Addie said, concerned. "Your grandpa can't abide a doctor, so for him to drive into St. John's . . ."

Nightingale set down her noodle necklace; I saw

my own fear cross her silent face. I knew what she was thinking—she was thinking same as me—*What if something bad had happened to Old Finn?* Old Finn was our only known family; the last one left to love us. If we lost him, we'd end up all alone. At eighty-three, Miss Addie was too old to raise three kids.

"Maybe we should wait," Nightingale said.

"No," I said, "by now, Old Finn ought to be home." Somehow facing down our troubles was always up to me. Baby was just six and Nightingale too timid. Old Finn always said it was the burden of the oldest to see the worst before everybody else, to be on the watch for trouble so the younger Stars stayed safe.

I put my finger in the dial and started with the three. 3-6-7. Everyone was watching; I couldn't hear a single breath. "But, Pride . . . ," Nightingale started like she wanted me to stop. Her serious black eyes were full of worry.

"Perhaps I should be the one to speak," Miss Addie offered weakly. She stood up from her chair and shuffled toward the phone.

"Okay," I said. I knew St. John's would tell a grown-up more about a fever, even if Miss Addie wasn't half as self-reliant as the Stars. Most days it was us who tended to Miss Addie.

We all sat there still as stone while we watched Miss Addie listen. "Oh dear," she finally said, and I heard in her hushed voice the news was bad. Baby snuggled close against my chest. "Well, yes, I'm the next of kin," Miss Addie answered, flustered. "Let me leave my number." *Next of kin* meant "family," but Miss Addie wasn't that. I couldn't believe Miss Addie had just lied. "All right," she said. "Thank you for your help."

She hung the heavy phone back on its hook, took a few long breaths like she was weighing how much trouble she ought to tell three kids. "I'm afraid," she said, a nervous warble rising in her voice. She fiddled with her wig of snowy ringlets. "Old Finn has some kind of infection. Some trouble with his brain."

"His brain?" Nightingale gasped. Old Finn's brain was full of history and Latin, algebra and physics, geography and ancient Greece. He had a head packed full of knowledge, some he tried to teach to us. Square roots, symphonies, and sonnets. "Old Finn can't lose his brain."

"Not lose." Miss Addie tried to say it cheerful, but still she wound her wrinkled hands into a knot. "Hopefully his trouble will just pass."

"But when's he coming back to Eden?" Baby asked. "Before we go to sleep?"

"Probably not," I said, because I knew the answer

without Miss Addie even saying. I rubbed my hand over Baby's soft brown bristles. Baby kept his head shaved like Old Finn, wore matching Wrangler jeans, cowboy boots they both bought at Newport Saddle. He'd been a miniature Old Finn ever since we moved to Eden.

"I imagine I'll have to keep you children here," Miss Addie said like she wasn't really certain.

"Here?" Baby's eyes grew huge. Miss Addie only had one narrow bed. There wasn't any place for us to sleep. The tiny trailer floor was covered with our crafts.

"But we're Old Finn's next of kin," Nightingale said, matter-of-fact. She was tucked up in the rocker, her knees up to her neck, her ruffled nightgown draped over her thin legs, her long black braids brushing her bare feet. "Why didn't you tell the truth?"

"Oh dear." Miss Addie shrugged, ashamed. "I didn't know what else to say." She shook her head like she wished she hadn't lied. "But when it comes down to you children, your grandpa doesn't want me passing information."

I thought about the visits from the county, how Old Finn worried every time that school woman came to check our lessons. Or how in Goodwell he'd walk away from questions he didn't like. *It's not anybody's business how we live at Eden,* Old Finn always said.

"Miss Addie's right," I said to Nightingale. "Old Finn wouldn't want a soul to know he's sick, or that we're left at Eden on our own. Even for one night."

"Maybe more," Miss Addie said as gently as she could. "We can't be certain what the future holds."

2

SELF-RELIANCE

Old Finn always joked he inherited Miss Addie—a retired, eccentric actress—as if she were some kind of keepsake his bachelor uncle, William Martin, left behind when he died and willed Eden to Old Finn. I only knew she'd been living on this land for years and years, long before Old Finn came from California; and when he made his home on William Martin's forty acres, Miss Addie just stayed put. Miss Addie and her craft projects and costumes, magazine and records, her little black-and-white TV, mounds of clutter that filled up most the trailer.

"I'm afraid I wasn't set for company," Miss Addie fussed when she woke up the next morning. She looked ancient in her housedress; shrunk down to bone with sags of pale, paper skin. I missed her layers of make-up, her strings of beads and bangles, the lively flowered muumuus she wore during the day. "I've only got a smidgen left of milk. One small dish of Wheaties."

"That's okay," I said. After a night on Miss Addie's scratchy carpet, one flimsy sheet spread over us all, I was ready to head home. "We have plenty at the cabin." I sat up, gave Nightingale a nudge. I didn't want Miss Addie to feel bad about the food; she'd already divided her last can of mushroom soup for supper. Filled us up on stale saltines. "Come on, Baby." I shook his little shoulder. "It's morning now, we need to head on home."

"Home?" Baby rubbed his eyes.

Nightingale pulled the sheet up to her chin. "Home without Old Finn?"

"You sure you children can fix breakfast for yourselves?" Miss Addie asked.

"I'm thirteen," I said. "Been thirteen for three weeks. And Nightingale's on her way to twelve. Plus breakfast is my job." We all had jobs at Eden; Old Finn had been preaching self-reliance since the first day that we came. Nearly two years straight of self-reliance lessons. Independence. Even though I'd been standing steady on my own two feet since the day I learned to walk. Still it was Old Finn's self-reliance that taught me how to fix a toilet, change a fuse, brew potato soup for supper, weed the garden, and chop wood. It's why we had our school at his table instead of going into Goodwell like everybody else. After all that training, I didn't need Miss Addie's

Wheaties to get by. "And until Old Finn gets done with his fever, we're going to have to practice independence, rise to the occasion." *Rise to the occasion* was Old Finn's famous phrase—it meant tackling a problem whether you wanted to or not.

"I'll rise!" Baby jumped up to his feet. "I'll fry up the sausage. Spread jelly on the toast. Shoot a squirrel for supper."

I laughed at that last part; Baby always had a dream to hunt.

"Miss Addie, why don't you come with us to the cabin?" Nightingale urged. Miss Addie hardly ever left her trailer. Like Old Finn, she was happiest at home. "You can be our family for today."

"Oh dear." Miss Addie sighed. "It's such a long walk on that wood path, and Lady Jane will frighten if I leave." Right now, Miss Addie's golden tabby was curled up in her lap, but mostly Lady Jane stalked mice in the meadow or dozed lazy on the hood of Old Finn's truck.

"Lady Jane won't mind it for one day," Nightingale argued. I could tell she didn't want to go back to our cabin without a grown-up along, even one as frail as Miss Addie. Nightingale wasn't ready to face Eden all alone.

* * *

It was sad and strange to cross the dewy meadow, to know the cabin would be empty, that Old Finn would be gone. Atticus and Scout grazed peaceful in the pasture, but Old Finn's shadow, Woody Guthrie, moped sad-eyed in the yard. "Oh no," I moaned. In the worry of the night, Woody Guthrie had gone without his supper. Summers Old Finn let the horses eat free off the land, but Woody Guthrie needed to be fed.

I called Woody Guthrie's name, gave a couple claps. Nightingale and Baby called him, too, but he just stayed there, staring; his spotted hound-dog head hung between his paws; his floppy ears draped on the ground like he didn't want to move an inch with Old Finn gone.

I ran ahead, left Nightingale and Baby to meander with Miss Addie; Miss Addie never moved too fast. Inside the silent cabin, Old Finn's coffee mug sat empty on the table, his dusty work boots stood beside the door. I grabbed Woody Guthrie's bowl and filled it with the last crumbs of broken kibble. Like Miss Addie's milk and Wheaties, Woody Guthrie's food was nearly gone.

I opened up the pantry. Old Finn's scribbled grocery list was taped up to the door. Friday was his shopping day in Goodwell, but when Friday came he'd barely left his bed. I added Miss Addie's milk and Wheaties, Woody Guthrie's Alpo.

I pulled the oatmeal from the cupboard, put a pan of water on to boil, set the bowls out on the table, poured Baby his milk. I was doing *first things first*, the way Old Finn always taught me. First I'd feed my family, then I'd ride to town for groceries. Groceries and a visit to St. John's.

3

MAKING DO

"I'm riding in on Atticus," I said. I ran the water on our dishes, scrubbed the film of fried egg from our plates. "I'll leave him at the Junk and Stuff with Thor, just the way I've done it with Old Finn." Now and then, Old Finn and I would set off for a ride, a time for just the two of us to talk. And Thor's place was the closest you could get a horse to town.

"Alone?" Miss Addie rubbed her neck. I was glad she'd painted makeup on her face, clipped on her emerald earrings, put on a bright green muumuu; she didn't look quite so fragile anymore. "But it's another mile at least from the Junk and Stuff to town. You'd have to walk that highway."

"I can do all that, Miss Addie," I said. "I've got to shop for groceries. Old Finn couldn't go on Friday, and you need your milk and Wheaties; Woody Guthrie's kibble is all gone."

"I'll go, too," Nightingale offered.

"You will?" I asked. Like Old Finn and Miss Addie,

Nightingale hardly ever wanted to leave Eden. "You've got to put on town clothes."

"I know." She frowned. Nightingale dressed in nightgowns the way other kids wore jeans. Flannel in the winter; cotton in the summer. Ruffled sleeves and fancy collars all year-round. And she was always in bare feet. She'd been that way since we were little; it's how Mama landed on that nickname: Nightingale. It was the word Nightingale gave the sleep gowns Mama sewed. "I want another nightingale," she'd beg. And Nightingale stuck.

When we moved in with Old Finn, he didn't make a stink about the nightgowns, so long as Nightingale put on clothes for town. It's why she went to Goodwell only for the library and ice cream, a visit to the doctor now and then.

"Me, too!" Baby said. "I'm going into Goodwell."

"I can't take you, Baby. Not today." I didn't want Baby with me at St. John's, not until I saw Old Finn myself. "You stay here with Miss Addie."

"Yes." Miss Addie patted his small hand. "I need a friend here, Baby."

While Nightingale climbed up to our loft to dig through clothes, I sat at the table to work with Old Finn's list. Some things he'd written, like liverwurst and rump roast, razor blades and Borax, could wait till he was well. Miss Addie knew exactly what she needed: Velveeta, macaroni, Wheaties, Wonder Bread, and milk. Seven different kinds of Campbell's soup. Oscar Mayer bologna. Gingersnaps and fresh saltines.

"I'm not sure what to buy," I told Miss Addie. "Old Finn makes the list; I just help him cook."

"It's easiest to think about the week," Miss Addie said. "Buy foods you can repeat like macaroni. That's the way I do and I get by."

"Food we can repeat?" I said to Baby.

"Chocolate cake!" he clapped.

"That does sound delicious," Miss Addie added.

I opened up Old Finn's Goodwell Baptist cookbook and found the recipe I used for chocolate cake. We had everything I'd need except for eggs; I'd fried the last of them for breakfast. "We're all out of eggs," I said. "But I can buy those at the Junk and Stuff from Thor."

"First we ought to figure out the money, Pride," Nightingale called down from the loft. "We'll need it to buy groceries."

I hadn't thought about the money; I only knew we needed food to eat. It was Nightingale who had the gift for numbers. Letters, too. Of all of us, she took to Old Finn's schooling best. While I was tending to the horses or working in the woodshed with Old Finn, Nightin-

14

gale balanced Old Finn's ledger, helped figure out the bills. She knew how money worked and where it went.

"Old Finn keeps ten dollars in the coffee can," she said. "But ten dollars won't go far."

I looked over at Miss Addie. Grown-ups had money. She could pay for food, just like she paid for movie magazines.

"I'm afraid I didn't earn much as an actress," Miss Addie said. "I write my list; your grandpa buys my groceries." I could tell she was embarrassed to have Old Finn buy her food. "But I never ask for much."

"You don't have any money?" Baby said. "Not a penny in your piggy bank?" Baby's piggy bank of pennies was a washed-clean tobacco tin.

"Just my two JFK half dollars I've saved as souvenirs. But I'd hate to spend my souvenirs for soup." Miss Addie kept her JFKs hidden in her closet in a tiny velvet box with Lovecraft Jewelry written on the top. Sometimes she'd take them out to give a look or remember JFK. I wasn't spending Miss Addie's souvenirs; I'd buy her groceries same as Old Finn did.

"We have ten at least," I said. "That ought to be enough."

I climbed up on the counter, opened up the highest cupboard where Old Finn's secret coffee can was kept.

Money for emergencies. One ten-dollar bill was folded up inside. "I'll just buy the little that we need. We've got potatoes in the pantry. Applesauce. Canned peaches we can eat."

"That's the spirit," Miss Addie said. "And I can go without the gingersnaps and crackers. Velveeta, too. I can eat my macaroni with a little dab of butter."

"Butter?" Baby said. "I used the last for toast."

Butter, I wrote down on my list. *Milk. Eggs. Bread.* We could live awhile on sugar sandwiches and eggs.